THE WRONG MAN TO LOVE

Samantha supposed her beloved godfather had known what he was doing when he left her the controlling shares in his huge department store—but how she wished he hadn't done it! For all it led to was her falling in love with Zachary Farrell, the new head of the business—who naturally had no time for her at all!

Books you will enjoy
by ROBERTA LEIGH

FLOWER OF THE DESERT

Working in Persia, Fleur had come to like and admire Persian ways—but she could never accept their attitude to women as mere chattels who should be content to marry and then be obedient to their husbands in all things. So she had better not fall in love with a Persian—least of all the attractive Karim Khan. But that was easier said than done . . .

GIRL FOR A MILLIONAIRE

'You'll be Cinderella with a clock that won't strike twelve for three whole weeks!' Christine assured Laurel when she persuaded her to come with her for a cruise in the Mediterranean on a millionaire's yacht. But this, Laurel soon found, was a rather rosy-coloured picture of it all—and when she met Nicolas Ponti she began to wish she had never come . . .

THE UNWILLING BRIDEGROOM

There was only one word for the method Melisande Godfrey had employed to force André Lubeck into marrying her: blackmail. She had been motivated solely by revenge, and had never paused to think what she would do once he *had* married her; certainly she hadn't expected to fall in love with him. And now, of course, he felt nothing for her but contempt . . .

MAN WITHOUT A HEART

Television personality Maxwell Lane was brilliant, powerful—and ruthless; and Andrea owed him a grudge for the way he had destroyed her uncle. She vowed to get her own back on him—and got an unexpected opportunity to do so. But then fate turned the tables on her in a way she had not expected . . .

THE WRONG MAN TO LOVE

BY

ROBERTA LEIGH

MILLS & BOON LIMITED
17–19 FOLEY STREET
LONDON W1A 1DR

First published 1977
Philippine copyright 1977
This edition 1977

ISBN 0 263 72506 5

Set in Linotype Pilgrim 10 on 11½ pt.

Made and printed in Great Britain by
Richard Clay (The Chaucer Press) Ltd., Bungay, Suffolk

CHAPTER ONE

SAMANTHA BYERS turned her back on the shore and walked back towards the grey stone house set at the foot of the softly rising hill. It was a misty Irish morning and the air sparkled with it and placed gentle drops of moisture on her long, soft fair hair. There was no curl in it, yet it did not lie limp, but had the lustre and shine of perfect health. There were droplets of moisture on the long, darker lashes that framed the grey eyes; eyes which were now warm with pleasure as the door of the house opened and an elderly man greeted her with a smiling 'Good morning.'

'You're up early, Uncle John.' It was a courtesy title, for he was no relation, merely a long-standing friend of her father's who still maintained his friendship with her mother and herself, even though her father had died several years ago.

'I was too restless to lie in bed,' he said in answer to her comment. 'Anyway, in London I'm always at the store by this time.'

'That's why you came to Ireland,' she reminded him. 'To get away from the store!'

'That's easier said than done. A big business gives one big problems.'

'Then sell up.'

He laughed. 'Just like that?'

'Why not? You have more money than you'll ever spend. I don't see the point in keeping on something that gives you worry.'

'I would have more worries if I sold out. Anyway, if you have a child and he is a problem to you, you don't disinherit him for that reason. Mind, I don't regard the store as a child,' he added, and Samantha laughed and shook her head, knowing this was exactly the way he regarded it. A widower and childless, John Farrell had built Farrells up from a small drapery shop into one of London's leading department stores. No wonder he regarded it as a living creation—despite what he said to the contrary. But it was also taking toll of his strength. She and her mother had been dismayed at how much he had aged in the three years since they had last seen him.

'You should come here more often, Uncle John,' she said, linking her arm through his and leading him into the kitchen where her mother was already making the breakfast.

'You shouldn't have moved out to the wilds of County Cork,' he grumbled. 'It beats me what a young girl like you finds to do here. And you too,' he said, turning to Mrs Byers, a sprightly woman of fifty who was at that moment heaping a plate with crisp curls of bacon and two fried eggs, sunny-side up.

'Eat that, John,' she said good-humouredly, 'and stop complaining about us because we don't conform to your ideas of living.' She set two plates of creamy porridge down for her daughter and herself. 'Samantha and I are both delighted that we moved here when Henry died. It's done wonders for my painting. I'm selling more today than I ever did when we lived in England—Samantha is a far better agent for me than the Stevens Gallery—and cheaper too! They used to take forty per cent commission.'

'And what do you take, Samantha?' John Farrell asked.

'Ten per cent.' Samantha smiled, showing perfect

white teeth behind a wide, charmingly shaped mouth meant for kisses and laughter.

'And you enjoy selling your mother's work?'

'I love every minute of it. It's as exciting as an adventure story. This year I've already been to America, Brussels and Oslo, and I'm off to Beirut next Wednesday. Mother is having a big exhibition there and we've already sold half the paintings before they've been hung!'

'Due to Samantha's wonderful ability to get the right people to look at my work,' her mother intervened. 'She's more than my agent, John, she's my biggest fan.'

'I thought *I* qualified for that description,' the man said in mock dismay.

'Art means nothing to you,' Mrs Byers said robustly. 'Your favourite picture is *The Stag At Bay*!'

He chuckled and settled down to his breakfast.

'I'll clear away,' Samantha said to her mother when the last cup of coffee had been served. 'You go up to the studio before you start champing at the bit.'

Without demur Mrs Byers did as she was told, but John Farrell remained where he was, sitting back in his chair, his eyes resting with affection on the tall slim figure of his goddaughter.

'I miss you and your mother very much,' he said quietly. 'That's the real reason why I objected to you both coming here.'

'I know.' Samantha half turned and gave him a smile before she continued to wash the dishes. 'But there's nothing to stop you coming out to see us as often as you like. I was serious when I suggested you gave up the store.' Hands in the soapy water, she turned again to look at him. 'Why don't you retire? I know your two nephews are in the business. Surely they can manage without you?'

'They can't wait to start,' he said, 'particularly Zack.

He's full of new-fangled ideas. He wants to cater for a wider market and double the size of the food department.'

'And his brother?'

'You mean Larry? He's Zachary's cousin, not his brother. He is the exact opposite. He would be happy to keep things the way they are—providing the profits don't drop—though as a matter of principle he always opposes everything Zachary wants to do.'

'Don't they like each other then?'

'Deep down they do. They grew up together. Larry's father was my youngest brother—he got killed racing—and my sister, Zachary's mother, brought Larry up as her own son. To all intents and purposes they are like brothers—and I suppose like brothers they have their differences.'

'One day you'll have to let them sort out things on their own,' Samantha commented, stacking the dishes on the draining board to dry. 'And it's silly to wait until you're old and ill before you retire. Why not do it now and come and live with us?'

John Farrell laughed. 'That's all you and your mother need—to look after an old man! No, I'm too set in my ways to change my life at this stage. I was born in harness and I'll die there.'

'Don't talk about dying.' Samantha came across the tiled floor and gave him a fierce hug. She had known John Farrell all her life and would always associate him with the happy days of her childhood.

'Do you really enjoy living here?' he asked quietly, 'or do you stay because of your mother?'

A shadow darkened the beautiful grey eyes. Looking into them, John Farrell was struck again by what a remarkably lovely looking girl Samantha was. Lovely. It was an apt word to describe her. Beautiful was too mundane an adjective to use, for she had a delicacy and softness that a casual onlooker might not notice. It took discerning eyes to appreciate Samantha, but when one did, there was ample reward to be found. She had her father's colouring and ascetic features, but where he had been tall and rangy, his daughter was tall and slender. Her hair was fairer too, bleached by the sun which had also lightly tanned her skin. There was a still quality about her that made him wonder whether this was the reason for her contentment here; made him wonder, too, how long this contentment would last if she were to fall in love. How old was she now? Twenty-two or three? Certainly it was time for her to settle down to a more positive way of life.

'Why the sigh?' she asked, breaking into his thoughts.

'I was thinking that your life wouldn't suit me. I know you travel a lot, but you're still stuck here too much. You should be meeting young men. Even be married by now.'

'All in good time,' she said with an easy smile. 'Come on, lazybones, help me in the garden.'

'I'm too old to do any weeding.'

'But not too old to rake the grass!'

Grumbling, he followed her out and a few moments later was happily employed pushing leaves into a pile.

At the end of the week he returned to London, declaring himself fitter than when he had arrived ten days earlier. A month after that Samantha departed for Beirut and throughly enjoyed the sophisticated atmosphere with which she was surrounded for the next fortnight. Her mother's exhibition was a success and by the time it closed not one painting was left unsold. She hadn't received any of her mother's usual chatty letters during her absence—apart from a brief note to say all was well—and though she knew that had anything gone amiss she would have heard at once, she felt an unusual disquiet that decided her against stopping over in London on the way back, and flew direct to Dublin instead.

It was evening when she arrived home and as soon as she entered the house she knew her premonition had been justified.

'It's John,' her mother explained. 'He died at the beginning of the week. I only returned yesterday from the funeral.'

Tears filled Samantha's eyes. 'Why didn't you let me know?'

'It would have been pointless for you to have flown back. I was only told myself after he had died. It was in his sleep.'

'That's a good way to go,' Samantha said slowly. 'I'm glad he didn't suffer. He would have hated to be ill and helpless.'

Mrs Byers nodded and looked as if there was something more to say. 'The lawyer had hoped you would be there for the reading of the will. I explained where you were and he agreed for me to stand in for you.'

'I hope Uncle John left me his chess set. He always said he would.'

'He didn't forget his promise.' Her mother smiled slightly. 'But he left you something much more important than that.'

Halfway up the stairs, Samantha stopped. 'Really? What was that?'

'Ten per cent of the shares in his company. Ten per cent of the voting stock,' she explained.

'The voting stock?' Leaving her case on the stairs, Samantha came slowly back to the hall. 'Tell me the rest, Mother. I can see from your face that there's more to it than that.'

'There is,' her mother agreed, and led the way into her

studio which took up one entire side of the house. This action told Samantha something serious was afoot. Whenever her mother had anything difficult to say she always retreated to her studio for reassurance. But where was the problem in owning ten per cent of the voting stock? It was a wonderful inheritance and totally unexpected.

'John left his two nephews forty-five per cent each,' Mrs Byers explained, 'which means that if they don't agree on policy *your* ten per cent can decide the issue. In other words, you are the lynch-pin.'

'Oh dear!'

'You can well say that,' Mrs Byers agreed. 'Neither of them are happy about it, as you can imagine. Zachary is furious.'

'He doesn't need to be. I have no intention of interfering. I know nothing about the way a store is run. In fact, I would be quite happy to sell my shares.' She stopped as she saw the look on her mother's face. 'Couldn't I do that?'

'You could if you wished, but that's exactly what John wouldn't want you to do.'

'Not even if I sold five per cent to each of his nephews?'

'It would still leave them in a position of stalemate. It would be worse, in fact, for there'd then be no one to try and keep the balance. And you couldn't sell your shares to a stranger because that would be even worse. John obviously had this in mind when he came out to see us.'

'To see *me*, you mean,' Samantha said. 'That must have been the purpose of the exercise: to decide what sort of a lynch-pin I would make.'

'He obviously thought you'd be a satisfactory one or he wouldn't have given you the all-important vote.' Mrs

Byers went over to her easel. 'He made another stipulation in his will—that you should work in the store for a year. It wasn't a demand, just a hope that you would. He felt if you worked in the various departments you would have a greater appreciation of the problems involved in running Farrell's.'

'You mean leave Ireland?'

'Temporarily.'

'What about you?'

'I'll stay on here. Mrs Halloran will be quite happy to live in and I have no shortage of friends who will be delighted to come out and stay with me. You needn't worry about me being lonely, Sam.'

'You seem very eager to have me leave,' said Samantha dryly.

'It's what John wanted,' Mrs Byers said, 'and he may be right. From your point of view it isn't good for you to live here so much. Anyway, before you make up your mind what you want to do with the stock—whether to keep it or sell it—you should learn as much about Farrells as you can.'

'I wish I had been at the funeral,' Samantha said slowly, 'though in a way I'm glad my last memory of Uncle John was of him being here. He was so happy that day in the garden, burning all the leaves.'

'And he's left another bonfire behind him,' Mrs Byers replied. 'With you in the centre of it!'

Samantha frowned. 'Do you think things will be that difficult?'

'They could be. But I'm sure that with your charm and diplomacy you'll be able to put out the fire!'

'Or get burnt at the stake for my efforts. Still, if the worst comes to the worst I can always give the shares to some lawyer and get him to act on my behalf. Then neither of John's nephews could complain of bias.'

'If John had wanted *that* he could have done it himself. He left that stock to you for a reason.'

'The hand ruling from the grave,' Samantha mocked wryly. 'I have a feeling Uncle John knew exactly what he was letting me in for.'

'Well, the quicker you go back to London and find out, the better. I suggest you rest up for a few days and then leave.'

CHAPTER TWO

SAMANTHA had stayed in London several times since she and her mother had gone to live in Ireland: accepting the hospitality of her closest friend, Jacqueline. But the apartment was too small for her to remain there any length of time and she knew she would have to find a place of her own.

'Furnished or unfurnished?' Jackie asked when Samantha had unpacked and settled in the spare room.

'Furnished. When my year is up in the store I shall probably go back to Ireland.'

'If you aren't married by then. Ten per cent of Farrell's makes you very eligible, you know.'

'Are you suggesting I'll be married for my money?' Samantha laughed.

'I'm suggesting you start to enjoy it and live it up a bit—that alone should bring you to the notice of all the young bachelors round about.'

'All!' Samantha flung her arms wide. 'I can see them clamouring at the front door to take me out.'

'I'm still stuck on Peter.' Jackie's *non sequitur* was spoken on a sigh. 'But unfortunately he isn't the marrying kind.'

Diplomatically Samantha was silent. Peter was a well-known political journalist whom Jackie had met when she had gone to work as his secretary. From the first moment they had clicked and her friend had not had eyes for any other man. But Peter, though he professed to love her, had made it plain he did not wish for marriage, though he seemed content to take no one out except Jackie and spent every evening with her when he was not occupied with his work.

'I'm not complaining,' Jackie said into the silence. 'I've loved my two years with Peter. I've had all the fun of marriage and none of the hassle. I only——' She stopped.

'I sense an implied "but" in your tone,' Samantha said with pretended casualness.

'You know very well there is. I *want* the hassle of marriage. I want the baby and the pram and having to queue at the supermarket. But I also know I won't get it from Peter. That's why I'm leaving.'

'Good for you. I'm sure you won't have any problem finding a job that's just as good.'

'It will take more than a change of job for me to forget Peter,' Jackie said, 'I'm leaving the country.'

Samantha was startled. 'Where are you going?'

'New Zealand. I have cousins out there and they're always inviting me to stay with them. Which is exactly what I'm going to do. If I like it, I'll stay there permanently.'

'Have you told Peter?'

'Yes. But he doesn't believe it.'

'You mean he thinks you won't go?'

'Oh, he knows I'll be leaving. I'm off in a fortnight, as a matter of fact. He just thinks I'll be back in a couple of months. But I won't. Even if I loathe it out there I'm not coming back to England until I've got over him.' She looked around her. 'Which brings me to this home, sweet home. I was going to sell off the rest of the lease, but if you'd like to——'

'Done!' Samantha interrupted jubilantly. 'I'm sorry you're going away, Jackie, but I'm delighted I can take over. This is exactly what I want. And of course if you do decide to come back, I'll hand it over to you again.'

'Don't tempt me,' said Jackie. 'I can't live all my life as Peter's girl-friend.'

'I didn't know you were pining for marriage,' Samantha said. 'You've always professed to love your independence.'

'I still do. But I don't see marriage as incompatible with that.'

'Obviously Peter does.'

'I know. He doesn't want the responsibility. Peter Pan, I call him.'

'When you've gone away he might grow up and realise how much he misses you.'

'I'm not banking on it.' Jackie lifted her shoulders. 'Anyway, let's not talk about me any more. Tell me what *your* plans are.'

'I've told you. Tomorrow I'm going to the store. I wrote to Zachary Farrell and his cousin and told them I'll be there.'

'I bet they'd like to cut your throat!'

'Thanks for reassuring me.'

Jackie grinned. 'There's nothing like knowing your enemies. They're bound to dislike you, Sam. So would I in their position. You're stopping either of them from getting control.'

'Surely that's better than having *one* of them in control?'

'One of them *must* have control—unless you intend sitting on the fence for ever?'

'Of course not.'

'That's why they'll both regard you as their enemy—until they know which one you're going to favour.'

'I don't intend to favour either of them,' Samantha stated. 'I want to remain unbiased.'

'Ha!' Jackie muttered. 'I've yet to meet a girl who can be unbiased when faced with two men. You're bound to prefer one to the other and that's going to affect your behaviour when it comes to any Board decision.'

'It's a possibility which I recognise,' Samantha conceded, 'though I don't intend to succumb to it. For Uncle John's sake I must think only of the store. That's why I need to know how it works.'

'Little Miss Tycoon!'

'You can laugh,' said Samantha, 'but it's unfortunately all too true.'

'Unfortunately, the girl says!' Jackie flung up her arms. 'You're the luckiest girl in the world. You'll have two young men sucking up to you to get your favour. If you——' She stopped. 'You wouldn't know if they're married, would you?'

'What difference does that make?'

'All the difference in the world. If they're single, having you as a wife would give them control.'

'A man wouldn't marry just for that.'

'Wouldn't he?' Jackie said dryly.

'I suppose he would, if he were ambitious and determined enough.' Samantha's eyes narrowed at the idea of this. 'But then I'm determined too, and when I marry it won't be in order to give someone the benefit of my voting stock!'

'Then let's hope that both the Farrell nephews are as

ugly as sin! That will be one way of helping you to remain unbiased.'

Samantha remembered this as she dressed for her meeting with them the next day. It had been arranged too early for her to have time to have her hair set, an action which she regretted, for no matter how business-like the clothes she wore, it was difficult to coax her hair into a style that complied with the image she wished to present.

'Leave it loose,' Jackie suggested. 'It's a good contrast with that Quaker outfit you're wearing.'

Samantha glanced down at her navy suit with its figure-fitting skirt and jacket. The severity of the line was softened by a deep blue chiffon blouse that gave a blue glow to her large grey eyes. 'I thought of putting my hair up into a French pleat.'

'That went out with the Ark. Leave it loose. You have beautiful hair and it's such a gorgeous colour.' Jackie sighed enviously. 'It's the sort that you can never get out of a bottle.'

Samantha smiled and ran a comb through the silky tresses. She coaxed the ends under with a brush, hoping it made her look less young than when they curled up into little duck's tails, and planted a small navy hat on her head.

'Is that supposed to make you look efficient?' Jackie asked.

'I always wear a hat for a business meeting,' Samantha replied, picking up her bag and gloves. 'I don't look scared, do I?'

'You look fighting fit,' Jackie assured her. 'And you'll have both those young men eating out of your hands within five minutes of meeting you.'

Samantha took heart from this comment as she found herself in the office that had once been Uncle John's and which now—if seating arrangements were anything to go by—had been taken over by Zachary Farrell. He was the one who sat behind the old-fashioned mahogany desk while his cousin Larry perched on the side of it. Both of them eyed her without expression, though Zachary's lack of it was more foreboding. But then he was a more foreboding-looking man than his cousin, being deep-voiced and stern-featured. It was difficult to judge his age, for he was sitting with his back to the light, and though she knew from her mother that he was in his early thirties, he could have been considerably older. His finely arched dark eyebrows were lowered over eyes whose colour she could not see from this angle and a slightly long, firm nose pointed down to a wide-lipped mouth. It was a mouth that did not suit the character she had given him. She could not help noting it and wondering what it would be like if it relaxed into a smile. Such a thought could not have been further from the mind of the man himself, for when he spoke his unusually deep voice held no hint of friendliness.

'You realise, of course, that my uncle's action came as a great surprise to my cousin and myself?'

'To me too,' Samantha said. 'I had no idea Uncle John was planning to do such a thing. He never mentioned it when he stayed with us in Ireland.'

Silence met this statement and glancing from the man behind the desk to the one seated upon it, she saw both faces exuding the same impression of disbelief.

'It's true,' she reiterated. 'Uncle John never breathed a hint that this was in his mind. If he had—if I'd known I would have tried to talk him out of it.'

'To discuss the might-have-been is pointless,' Zachary Farrell said. 'We must now decide how we proceed in the future. Ideally you should sell your shares to my cousin and myself.'

'Half each?'

'Naturally I would prefer to have them all,' he said without a hint of humour, 'but since my cousin is of the same opinion, we would reach a position of stalemate. But if you gave us each five per cent...'

'If Uncle John had wanted that, he wouldn't have left me the shares in the first place.' Samantha moved forward in her chair to sit up more primly. Her skirt moved as she did, showing a slightly longer expanse of shapely leg. It attracted the attention of the man perched on the edge of the desk, and he fixed it with a pair of brown eyes which were suddenly alert.

'I'm not saying I won't eventually do that,' she continued, 'but for the moment I would rather follow Uncle John's wishes.'

'Wishes?' Zachary Farrell queried.

'That I should work in the store for a year and learn how the business is run.'

'One needs to have more than a day-to-day working knowledge of the store to know how Farrell's operates,' he said bleakly. 'To do that you require business acumen and flair.'

Irritated, she stared across the desk at him and wished she were not directly facing the light, for it gave him an advantage over her.

'How do you know I don't have that kind of flair?'

'What were you doing before you came here?' he asked. Seeing her expression he gave a smile—if such a word could be used to describe the derisive way in which one side of his mouth turned up.

'I think it's very commendable of Miss Byers to want to follow Uncle John's will.' Larry Farrell spoke for the first time. 'And since we're all in the family, so to speak, I suggest we drop the Mr and Miss.' His smile was a genuine one, appreciative of the way the sun was turning her hair into a golden aureole around her head. 'Which Department are you planning to start in, Samantha?'

She was startled. 'I hadn't thought that far ahead.'

'Flowers, I think. You will outshine all the blooms there!'

'I suggest Miss Byers begins in Hardware,' Zachary Farrell spoke in a tone which indicated that he wished it was Hard Labour.

'Surely Samantha can do better than that to start with?'

'If that's where I'm needed,' Samantha said at once, 'that's where I'll go.'

'You're not needed anywhere,' Zachary Farrell said. 'But since you wish to comply with my uncle's wishes ...'

'When can I start?' she asked, rising so as not to give him the opportunity of making a move first.

'Why not tomorrow?' His tone was bland. 'The store opens at nine, but you needn't be here before eight-fifty.'

'That will suit me perfectly.' Her tone was equally bland. 'Do I have to wear a uniform?'

'Any simple garment in black or navy will do. You wear a badge, of course. I will tell the Manager of the Department to expect you. Do you wish me to let them know you are one of the owners of Farrell's?'

She knew instantly that to say yes would make him think she was taking the easy way out; and though she knew that by saying no she was playing into his hands, she had no option but to do it. She shook her head, and the way in which his mouth turned up in the semblance of a smile confirmed her suspicions. What an unlikeable man he was! She found it hard to understand why Uncle John had found it difficult to make up his mind which one of his nephews should be given control of his store.

For herself she would have had no such problem. Larry Farrell would have won hands down.

'I will have to give the Department Heads some reason why you're going from one section to another.' Zachary Farrell was speaking again. 'Normally a Personnel Officer would interview you and decide where you would be most suitable.' He frowned. 'I'll have to think of something.'

'I'm sure you can.' Murmuring goodbye, she went into the corridor and had not yet reached the lift when the younger of the cousins came after her.

'Why the rush?' he asked. 'I would like us to get better acquainted. After all, we are all working partners together.'

'Partners?'

'Naturally. Your vote is crucial to the running of the company. This whole vast edifice——' he waved his hands around him— 'which employs several hundred men and women, to say nothing of giving further employment to thousands in the factories, is controlled by three people—Zachary, myself and you. Because of that, it's important for us to understand and like each other.'

'I can't see your cousin liking me.'

'Don't take any notice of Zachary's manner. His father was Polish, and you know how moody Poles can be!'

'Farrell isn't a Polish name,' she said, surprised.

'His father's was something unpronounceable. He died when Zack was ten and Uncle John suggested he take the family name.'

This gave Samantha another reason for disliking him. How typical of him to take the name of the man whose department store he had hoped to own, rather than to remain loyal to the name of his father.

'Join me for coffee,' Larry Farrell said and, seeing her silence as acquiescence, put his hand under her arm and guided her past the lift into a room further along the corridor.

It was not as large as the one they had left, but furnished in a more modern manner, which made it look friendlier. The leather easy chairs were the latest in Italian design, the carpet was thick underfoot and there was a television set in one corner. Larry caught her eyeing it and grinned.

'Zack gets mad with me every time he sees it,' he confided. 'But I like to watch the racing.'

'And listen to music too,' she said demurely, noticing the stereo on the shelf behind him.

'If I'm working late and I'm alone.'

She could not imagine either occurrence happening to him and was curious to know how active a part he took in the running of the store.

'Coffee or something stronger?' he asked.

'Coffee would be lovely. And some biscuits if possible. I'm starving.'

'Would you like something more substantial?'

'No, thanks. Biscuits will be fine. But I'm used to having breakfast and I was late out of bed this morning and only had orange juice.'

'Don't tell me you're an egg and bacon girl.'

'And toast and marmalade too!'

'You must have hollow legs.' He eyed her shapely limbs appreciatively.

'Just an active metabolism.' Because he looked as if he would like to pursue the subject, she said hastily: 'Do you and your cousin have specific tasks here, Mr Farrell?'

'Zachary is in charge of the overall buying and the running of the store, while I look after Personnel and Publicity.'

Because of her limited knowledge of the way a department store worked, she did not know if this was a fair division of labour. Somehow she did not think it was, and the young man's next words proved her to be right.

'I would like to do more,' he said, 'but Zach won't let me. Anyway, if I make any decision without his approval, he overrides it—even if he subsequently gives in. He loves to make out that he's the boss.'

'But you're both equal,' she said.

'I know. But I like a quiet life. Arguments consume too much of one's energy.'

'If Uncle John had wanted your cousin to be in charge,' she said, 'he would have given him control. Doesn't that make you want to stand up for yourself and your own ideas?'

'Occasionally,' Larry Farrell admitted. 'But I lack the determination to fight.'

'Don't you care what happens to the store?'

'Of course I do. But unlike Zachary and my uncle, I've always thought there are other things equally important. Things like enjoying one's life and working in a job that means something to you.' He hesitated. 'From which you may gather that my ambitions don't lie in Farrell's of Piccadilly.'

She nodded and waited for him to say more. Before he could do so, a middle-aged secretary came in with coffee and biscuits.

'Mrs Evans, you must be psychic!' As she set down the tray he introduced her to Samantha. 'You had better arrange for Miss Byers to have an office. Mr Zachary's old one, I think.'

'I'd better check with Mr Zachary first.'

'There's no need to do that. He won't be going back to it now.'

Mrs Evans looked unconvinced but did not demur,

though Samantha was sure she still intended to obtain Zachary Farrell's permission before doing anything about it.

'Will I need an office?' Samantha asked Larry.

'Naturally. As a working director you will be expected to have one.'

'Are there only the three of us?'

'We have a large Board of Directors,' he replied, 'but *our* votes are the only ones that count in any policy-making decisions concerning the running of the store. Hence your importance to Cousin Zachary.'

'And to you too,' she added. 'I don't believe you're as easy-going as you pretend.'

'I'm not easy-going in the things that matter to me,' he smiled. 'Besides which I never fight if I know I can't win. And no one could win against Uncle or Zack. But now that it's you and me——'

'You and me and your cousin,' she intervened quickly. 'I'm neutral, Mr Farrell. Please remember that.'

She had asserted to her mother and to Jackie that she intended to be unbiased and form her own opinions of these two men, and though she had already started to form one of Zachary Farrell, she refused to let it solidify into anything as strong as dislike. After all, some people did not come out well at a first meeting, especially if they were on the defensive, as he had obviously been. She could not blame him for it either. In his position she might well have felt the same. As for Larry Farrell . . . his charm was meaningless and merely indicated that he was better at simulating than his cousin. No, she must tread the middle path for much longer before going down one side or the other. If she ever did.

It was not until she was standing outside the store with him, while the commissionaire flagged down a taxi, that she saw the charm in full operation.

'As you've been living in Ireland so long, you won't have a home in London, will you? So why not let Farrell's find you an apartment? We have our own Estate Agency.'

'I'm taking over a friend's place. I've been very lucky.'

'I'm glad.' He smiled. 'I assume the telephone isn't in your name?'

'You assume right.' She climbed into the taxi and he grinned at her through the open window.

'Until tomorrow, Samantha. I'll be down to see you once you've settled in.'

'What exactly will I have to do?' she asked.

'Just learn how the Department is run. The Department Manager will tell you all about it.'

As the taxi drew out into the stream of traffic, Samantha realised that if she worked in the store incognito, she would be judged on merit alone. And as she was totally without experience, merit might be a long time coming. Zachary Farrell knew this, of course, and no doubt intended to make her sojourn at the store as uncomfortable as he could. How bitterly he resented her having a controlling block of shares, and how foolish of him to show his resentment so blatantly. Still, had he been charming she would have suspected him of Machiavellian subtlety. She half smiled. Subtlety was not his forte—the way he had behaved this morning had proved *that* beyond all doubt. But at least she knew where she stood with him and, as her mother frequently said, it was better to know where the devil was than to try and guess where he might be hiding.

CHAPTER THREE

AT a quarter to nine the next morning Samantha presented herself at the front entrance of Farrell's. The door was locked and a uniformed man inside looked at her oddly and pointed to the left. After a few seconds' thought, she correctly interpreted this as being a signal to another entrance. Naturally there would be a separate one for the staff. It had been stupid of her not to have known.

She hurried along the pavement. Farrell's occupied an entire block and by the time she found the right door it was exactly nine o'clock. Even then it took her a few more moments to reach the lower ground floor and the Hardware Section, which seemed to be a vast one. Assistants were already removing covers from some of the counters and putting loose cash in the various tills. Samantha looked around her uncertainly, not sure if any of them was the Manager and wondering how soon he would put in an appearance.

'You're new here, aren't you?' A young man came up to her. He wore a dark suit and had the Farrell badge in his lapel.

She nodded. 'I'm waiting to see the Manager of the Department.'

'He isn't due in until nine-thirty. I'm his assistant. Maybe I can help you?'

She was sure Zachary Farrell had not spoken to him about her and she shook her head. 'I'll wait for the Manager.'

Disappointed, he went away and, unwilling to remain the focal point of interested male stares, Samantha wandered around the floor. Half of it was given over to a large Do-It-Yourself section. This surprised her, for Farrell's had the reputation of being highly priced with a wealthy clientele. Then she noticed that many of the products sold were foreign and expensive and not to be found in any other shop in London. It seemed that even in Do-It-Yourself, Farrell's went in for the best. She thought it was a good idea to have this sort of section, for these days everyone was interested in cutting costs, no matter how rich they were.

'Miss Byers?' A middle-aged man was bearing down on her, hand extended. 'I'm Mr Carstair. Mr Farrell has spoken to me about you. I'm sorry I wasn't here when you arrived, but I didn't expect you as early as this.'

'I was told staff had to be here by a quarter to nine.'

'That wouldn't apply to you, Miss Byers,' he said hastily, lowering his voice. 'Mr Farrell has explained to me about the book you're planning to write and I'm delighted you wish to get first-hand experience. So many authors rely on their imagination when it comes to facts! Hardware is an excellent place to begin. Until recently it was the most underestimated section in the store. But since Mr Farrell has taken an interest in us, our turnover has trebled.'

'Taken an interest in it?' she queried. 'What do you mean?'

'By giving us room to expand. Old Mr Farrell didn't like this section at all. It was Mr Zachary who believed that people—wealthy ones, I mean—were becoming interested in doing their own home improvements. And he's been proved right, too. Yes, indeed he has. And the more new things we can offer for sale, the more we'll expand.'

'You've got some wonderful gadgets,' said Samantha. 'I've been admiring them.'

'We've Mr Zachary to thank for it. He's doing all the buying himself. It's a mammoth task and I don't know how he finds the time.'

Samantha found it strange that Zachary Farrell should concern himself with buying for one of his Departments and wondered if he were the sort of man who hated to delegate authority. He surely did not run the whole store this way? Even a man of formidable energy would find it impossible. But it would be unwise to question Mr Carstair on this point and she made a mental note to find out some other way.

Larry gave her the answer when he came in search of her at mid-morning to take her into the Health Bar for a fortifying fruit juice sundae.

'Uncle John used to bring me here when I was a little girl,' she said, feeling a pang of regret that such a treat would never again be hers. 'It wasn't called a Health Bar then. Something more like Coffee Bar.'

'We had to move with the times,' Larry said, 'and this was Uncle John's big step forward. Mind you, it broke his heart to take out all the walnut panelling and install steel and glass. But Zachary insisted. He said if one were going to break with the old tradition, then it had to be a complete break.' He sipped his guava juice and eyed a passing trolley of nut cakes and fruit tarts.

'Where do the staff go for their mid-morning break?' she asked.

'Not here,' he assured her. 'Zachary doesn't even like the Directors to come in here. The staff have their own canteen in a new building on the other side of the road. There's an underground passage to it so that you don't have to go outside. That's one reason why Zachary wants to buy the whole building across the way. He'd like to build a rooftop gallery to lead into it.'

'You sound as if you don't like the idea.'

'I don't. I think we're big enough.'

'What did Uncle John think?'

'I don't know. Zachary only sprang this idea on the Board a few weeks ago. There'll be a fight over it.'

'I hope not.' She was dismayed at thc prospect. 'I wouldn't want to veto something—or agree it either—unless I knew exactly what I was doing.'

'You can always refuse to use your casting vote and leave me and Zachary to fight it out.'

'Yesterday you said you didn't fight.'

'That was yesterday,' he smiled.

'A character as strong as shifting sand,' she murmured.

'So my enemies say!' He pointed to her empty glass and, at her nod, ordered it to be refilled. 'But I also said yesterday that I fight for the things I believe in. And right now I believe we should consolidate. Expansion can come later.'

'Talking of the word later reminds me to be getting back to work.' She rose hurriedly.

'Don't be silly,' Larry smiled. 'You aren't one of the staff.'

'I told your cousin that I want to be treated as if I am.'

'More fool you. Once you let him start on the boss syndrome, he doesn't know where to stop.'

She forbore to tell him that his cousin had told Mr Carstair to let her do exactly as she liked—a fact which had surprised her as much as she knew it would surprise Larry—and instead began to walk to the exit.

'Unfortunately I'm not free for lunch,' Larry said in her ear, 'but I'm quite frcc for dinner. I hope you are?'

She hesitated, then nodded. There was no reason why she should not go out with him.

'I'll call for you at eight,' he continued. 'What's your address?'

She gave it to him and he wrote it down in a small fat notebook which, she was sure, was full of other girls' names. Even without being a Farrell, Larry would have no shortage of female company, for he was good-looking and markedly debonair. That was the exact word to describe his smoothly brushed light-brown hair, his fair skin and twinkling brown eyes. Though she was tall, he topped her by six inches and had a frame to which his well-cut suit did justice. Yes, Larry Farrell was a good-looking young man and knew it.

'Until eight,' he said, and touched her lightly on the arm before leaving her.

For the rest of the day she was kept busy serving customers and, in the brief moments of respite, examined the stock on display. The assistants were expected to know a great deal about the articles they were selling and lectures were given to explain some of the more elaborate mechanical objects. One such lecture was being held this evening, half an hour before the store closed, and Mr Carstair suggested she might like to attend.

At five o'clock she hurried along to the lecture hall, which turned out to be a large room with a dais and screen at one end. Here, a technician had fitted up the object he was going to talk about and he explained in detail how it worked. Tonight it was a drill and wood cutter, sufficiently light for a woman to use with ease. He was easy to follow and at the end of the lecture, when he paused to answer questions, Samantha asked him why the written instructions that came with the machine were so much more difficult to understand than his own explanation had been.

'I don't know,' he admitted. 'But I've already taken it up with the firm and new instructions are being printed.'

'Do you think they could let us have them to put into existing stock?'

'I'll make a note of it,' he promised.

'And also to send out to those clients who have already bought one of these drills? Most of our clients have accounts here,' she added, 'so we'd have their addresses.'

He nodded again and she sat down, noticing that a few of the staff were eyeing her curiously. She wished she had not spoken up. Still, she was here to learn and if this meant asking questions, then so be it.

Shortly before five-thirty the lecture ended. The closing-time bell had not yet rung, but Samantha did not think it worth while to return to her Department and went instead to collect her outdoor things from the staff cloakroom. Tomorrow she would bring in a pair of flat-heeled shoes. Standing in high-heeled ones had made her feet ache and she hoped Larry had only meant dinner when he had suggested it, and did not also have dancing in mind.

Tiredly she made her way to the exit and was walking to the bus stop when a small dark car moved along the kerb in time with her. She glanced at it, her step faltering as she recognised Zachary Farrell behind the wheel.

'Get in,' he ordered.

Glancing round surreptitiously, she did so.

'Why the guilty look?' he asked bluntly.

'I thought it would look odd if any of the staff saw me getting into your car.'

'They're used to seeing girls getting into Larry's,' he said, dryly, setting the car in motion again. 'Where do you live?'

'Near Harrod's.'

'Convenient for shopping.' His voice was still dry.

'I wouldn't shop there.' Her tone matched his. 'My

loyalties belong entirely to Farrell's.'

'You also get a discount from us,' he said.

'Do I?' He shot her a look of suspicion and she controlled her temper. 'I didn't know that, Mr Farrell. Thanks for telling me. Does that apply to everything I buy?'

'Everything—though the discounts vary. The family get a larger discount than anyone else.'

'The privilege of being a Farrell,' she murmured.

'The privilege of being able to *run* Farrell's,' he corrected.

'Do you see it as your life's work?' she asked.

'Yes.' His voice was curt. 'We cater to a need and provide a service. I like the word service, Miss Byers, though in this day and age it seems to be going out of fashion. That's why I want to make sure Farrell's carries on. We serve the public and there is no shame in serving—as long as it is done with pride.'

Samantha was moved by the words, for they brought back many memories. 'When you speak in that way, it's like hearing Uncle John.'

'He brought me up.'

'I thought you grew up with Larry?'

'Only for a few years. When Uncle Tony died—Larry's father—Uncle John stepped in as our father figure. Or perhaps I should say as *my* father figure.'

'Your father was Polish, wasn't he?'

'You seem to know a lot about me?' He swerved to avoid a car which had pulled out ahead of him without warning.

'Only what people have told me,' she replied defensively. 'I didn't ask questions about you.'

'I wouldn't mind if you did. I'm prepared to go around asking questions about *you*. It's important that we understand each other.'

'To know isn't always to understand.'

'I hope it *will* be in our case.' His hands gripped the wheel and she felt he was gearing himself to say more. 'I would like to begin by having dinner with you tonight,' he went on. 'I'm sorry it's such short notice.'

'I'm afraid I'm not free. I—as a matter of fact I'm having dinner with Larry.'

'My quick-off-the-mark cousin,' he said sarcastically.

'He only preceded you by a few hours!'

'I'm not criticising him; merely making a comment.'

'I'm free tomorrow,' she said, not wishing him to think she was showing any preference.

'Unfortunately I'm not. Nor any other night this week.'

They were driving down Sloane Street and she directed him to her apartment, which was in an anonymous block off Lowndes Square.

'Did you live here before you went to Ireland?' he asked.

'Good heavens, no. You would never get my mother into anything except a house. We had a big rambling one in Maida Vale.'

'Uncle John said your home in Ireland is charming.'

'It is.' She looked him full in the face. 'You must come and visit us some time.'

'Is that a sometime invitation?' He saw her puzzlement and added: 'Some time, never.'

'Oh no!' She went pink. 'It was a genuine invitation.'

His mouth lifted at the corners. Both corners this time, she noted, turning it into a real smile and making him look younger than his age.

She stepped out of the car and, to her surprise, he got out with her, extending his hand to say goodbye. It was the first time she had stood next to him and in her high heels his eyes were only a couple of inches above hers.

Yet because of his broad chest he gave an impression of greater height, though he was not more than five foot ten. She was also close enough to see the colour of his eyes which, considering the darkness of his hair, were surprisingly light and a similar grey to her own. But his were more noticeable, being set in a swarthy-skinned face. She had always considered Poles to be fair by race and was curious to know more of his background.

'Your expression gives away your thoughts.' His voice was so deep that she had to strain to hear it, particularly since he had made no attempt to raise it above the noise of the rush hour traffic. But no doubt he rarely had the need to speak loudly; he looked as if he were used to people listening to him with attention.

'I was thinking how dark you were,' she said. 'I mean considering you're half Polish.'

'The borders of Poland extend over a large area,' he said wryly. 'My ethnic origins may not be pure Slav.'

'You're rather the way I remember Uncle John. When I was a child his hair was as black as yours.'

The man in front of her half smiled, then abruptly shook her hand and returned to his car. It seemed small for him and she was surprised he did not drive a bigger one. Carefully he pulled out into the stream of traffic. He did not look round at her and she went into her apartment. Why hadn't he suggested another night for their dinner? Was he annoyed that she had not been free tonight? Curious to know with whom he was engaged for the rest of the week, she went into her bedroom and dropped her coat on a chair. That was something she was sure to learn from Larry. He was a garrulous man and, as his main topic of conversation was his cousin, she expected this evening to be an informative one.

Larry arrived promptly to time, his expressive face showing appreciation of her appearance. Yet she knew that had she looked like the back of a bus he would still have been charming to her and taken her out. It's the voting shares I hold, that *he* would like to hold, she thought with amusement, and warned herself to remember this. Yet she did not care if his liking for her was not genuine. He was a good-looking escort, but she could never be serious about him. It was strange how clearly she knew this. The certainty of it made her wonder what mechanism in one person could trigger off a response in another, so that you could tell, almost from the word go, that a deeper emotion would result.

Yet so far no one had triggered an emotional response in her. She had time to spare, of course, but she still felt she was missing out on something. Perhaps it was because many of her friends were already married and Jackie, her closest one, had been seriously in love for two years. But nothing had come of Jackie's love; that was one more thing to remember.

As she had anticipated, Larry took her to an excellent restaurant. Champagne was already on ice and it was opened for them as soon as they sat down.

'What are we celebrating?' she asked.

'Our first dinner together. The first of many.'

She drank to the toast, aware of the women in the room who were looking in their direction and no doubt envying her the good-looking man who was making it plain he had eyes for no one except herself.

Larry was an attentive escort and a master in the art of the subtle compliment. Many of them he left half said, completing them with his eyes, and when they danced, he held her close enough to show he would have liked to hold her closer still, indicating—by the fact that he did not do so—that he also held her in respect. Larry was obviously expert at making a girl feel great.

To her surprise he did not refer to his cousin until they

were sipping their coffee, and only did so then because she brought his name into the conversation by saying he had asked her to dine with him that night.

'I bet his nose was out of joint when you refused,' Larry grinned. 'I'm glad I beat him to it.'

'I hope you're not taking me out just to spite your cousin?' she mocked. 'I suspect an element of competition between the two of you.'

'Zachary's girl-friends aren't my type.'

'I can't imagine him having any. He seems too serious.'

'He's still a man!' Larry grinned. 'He's a love 'em and leave 'em man.'

'Like you,' she added.

'Am I?' He put on a pained expression though his eyes were twinkling.

'You know you are. That's one of the nice things about you. You flirt, but you make it obvious you're flirting. If a girl allows herself to get serious over you, she'll only have herself to blame.'

'You seem to have formed a pretty definite opinion of my character on a couple of short meetings,' he said. 'Or am I so easy to read?' He held up his hand. 'Don't answer that. Whatever you say, I'm bound not to like it!'

She shrugged acceptance of this. 'Haven't you or your cousin wanted to get married?'

'Speaking for myself, no. Until now I never felt the need. I think Zachary has felt the same way, though if he goes on seeing Marie he'll have to make up his mind one way or the other.'

'Is she his latest?'

'His latest and longest. They've been together for two years, so he must be pretty serious about her. Normally they come and go with him—the way they've done with me.'

'Don't you get tired of playing the field?'

He laughed. 'What a question to ask a man!'

'I don't see why,' she persisted. 'Surely there comes a time when you only want to be with one particular woman?'

'You mean when the possessive instinct takes over and you can't rest until you've made the girl legally yours?'

She sipped her champagne. 'You make it sound very physical.'

'It is. That's why most marriages take place: because of a man's desire to keep other men away from his own pot of honey! Women marry for different reasons,' he added. 'Either they're scared of losing their looks and being left old and alone, or they're worried about their earning power and have a need for security. Sometimes it's a combination of both.'

'I could argue with you on this subject all night,' she said crossly.

'What a waste of a night!'

'Does your cousin think the way you do?' she asked.

'I guess so. It isn't something we've discussed. Old Zack's not very communicative, you know. He plays his cards so close to his chest that sometimes I don't think he even lets himself see them! He was like that even as a kid.'

'Were you resentful when he came to live with you?'

Larry shook his head. 'He's four years older than me and that gave him the advantage of knowing a lot of things I didn't. He taught me how to row and to dive and during our school holidays he'd always let me tag after him.'

'So you really did grow up like brothers?'

'I guess so. I've never given it much thought.'

Samantha knew he was being truthful and decided that his attitude to his cousin was his most likeable characteristic. Other boys might have been jealous at having to share their home and parents with another child, yet it had not apparently disturbed Larry. Such an attitude stemmed from a deep-rooted sense of security which could either have come from his parents or from his own belief in himself. From what she knew of him, she judged it to be a bit of both.

'Did you grow up knowing you would both inherit Farrell's?' she asked.

'It was something we took for granted, though I think that deep down I always thought it would be Zachary's. His mother was Uncle's John's twin sister, so by right of inheritance it should have been his.'

'Your uncle obviously didn't think so.'

'I know. He was scrupulously fair. He never differentiated between us. It was the only time when his business acumen let him down!' Larry saw her startled look and raised his eyebrows in a wry movement. 'Businesswise, Zachary is way ahead of me. If my uncle had let his head rule his heart, he would have given Zachary control. But he was so determined not to show favouritism that he brought you into the picture instead.'

'Uncle John's little weakness,' she said slowly.

Larry chuckled. 'That's a good way of putting it.' He gave her a frank look. 'When I first heard what he'd done, I laughed. I thought he'd turned the tables on us and was forcing us to work together amicably.'

'And what do you think now?'

'That we don't need to worry. After all, you're here to make an unbiased third.'

'As long as you remember that,' she said bluntly. 'I would never allow personal liking to cloud my business judgment.'

His eyes mocked her. 'How knowledgeable is that business judgment of yours, my fair-haired Samantha?'

'Knowledgeable enough to know its limitations—which is why I'm following Uncle John's suggestion and working in the store. Until I've got myself some experience I intend to maintain a very low profile. So don't think you can charm me into siding with you.'

'I knew you suspected my motives for asking you out,' he said reproachfully. 'And I won't deny it because I know you won't believe me. Instead, I'm going to let time talk for me.' His head tilted to one side. 'You will let me see you again, won't you?'

'Every day at Farrell's!' Before he could add anything to this, she went on, 'Of course I'll see you again. You're fun to be with.'

'So are you. How come you're still single? I'd have thought someone with your beauty and brains would have been snapped up long ago?'

'Perhaps all the men I've known have been like you and your cousin—playmates and not keepmates!'

He chuckled. 'I can easily see a man wanting to be *your* keepmate.'

She shrugged. 'Actually I've never fallen in love.'

'No black-haired prince on a white charger?'

'Not even a redhead on a palomino!'

He laughed outright. 'When I first heard of you I wondered if you were a free-living liberationist—bearing in mind your arty background. I think I thought wrong!'

'You certainly did. My mother was as good with a hairbrush as a paintbrush! I was very strictly brought up.'

'What's it like to have a famous parent?'

'Great fun. And I genuinely admire what she does; which makes it even more fun.'

'I'm a fan of hers too. I always like pictures to resemble reality. Abstract stuff leaves me cold.' He refilled their coffee cups. 'I wouldn't go out and buy a painting, though. I'm just as happy with a print.'

She was not overly surprised at his attitude but said politely: 'You probably have a very good eye for what you like.'

'Zachary is the one who knows about art,' Larry said. 'His house is full of paintings.'

'Don't you live together?'

'What an idea! We haven't done so for years. We each have our own pad in town and Zack used to spend his weekends at Uncle John's place in the country.'

'I remember going there a few times when I was a child,' Samantha murmured.

'It belongs to Zack now. Uncle left it to both of us, but I was happy to sell my half. I'm not the squire type.'

Samantha could not see Zachary Farrell in the role either, but knew that if she said so, Larry would see it as a criticism of his cousin. And she must not show herself to be critical of either of them. At least not until she knew much more about the way the store was run. And about the two Farrells themselves, she added.

This last thought came into her mind again as Larry drove her home, kissed her lightly on the brow and wished her goodnight. This particular branch of the family tree was delightful and easy to know on the surface, but she would be unwise to assume there were no prickly thorns behind the leaves. Soberly she went up to her apartment. Life ahead was going to be interesting, but it was also going to be difficult.

CHAPTER FOUR

AFTER working for two weeks in the Hardware Department, Samantha was delighted to receive word from Zachary's secretary that she was expected in the Art Department the following Monday. This was far more her milieu and when she said as much to Larry, he expressed surprise that she had bothered to work in Hardware at all, feeling the way she did.

'But Uncle John specifically said he wanted me to work in every Department,' she explained. 'Not just the ones to which I'm drawn by inclination.'

'If that was the case, you'd probably end up in Jewellery or Clothes!' he teased.

'Or Furs,' she retorted, and then immediately shook her head. 'No, not Furs. I think mink looks much better on a mink!'

His laugh was loud and people at the next table looked across at them. They were dining in the same restaurant to which he had taken her the first time they had gone out. In the last fortnight Samantha had seen him four times, not counting the odd occasions when he popped in during the day to see how she was getting on. Though she kept telling herself not to read too much into his attentions, she could not help thinking he was genuinely attracted to her.

'Why shouldn't he be?' Jackie had said when she had mentioned it. 'You're a stunning-looking girl. Peter's always remarking on it.'

'Praise indeed,' Samantha had said dryly.

'Coming from Peter, it is. In his kind of job, women fawn all over him.' Jackie had sighed deeply. 'I wonder if

I'm doing the right thing in leaving him?'

'You're doing the right thing for your future,' Samantha had said firmly. 'You've told him you're going away and you can't back down now. Give yourself a chance to make a new life.'

Jackie had tried to look bright at the prospect but had failed dismally, and her departure for the airport the next day had been a tearful one, particularly as Peter had been unable to see her off because of an unexpected assignment to Helsinki.

'But he still believes I'll be back in a couple of months,' Jackie had stated.

'Prove him wrong,' had been Samantha's final words to her friend and, waving her goodbye when she had gone through the departure gates, she had prayed fervently that Jackie would not weaken.

It was strange to return to the apartment and know she would not be sharing it with anyone. It suddenly seemed twice as large and far emptier. But she did not regret taking it and knew that with room to spare she would be able to put more of her own things around her. A couple of her mother's paintings in the sitting room, for instance, to replace the prints which Jackie had put there, and a delicate Dégas pastel on the wall opposite her bed, so that she would see it each morning when she awoke. It seemed to her like an omen that, with her mother's pictures hung and other objects of sentimental value placed in the sitting room, she should go to Farrell's the next morning and start work in the Art Department. The atmosphere here was quite different from the plebian one of the lower ground floor, and after a couple of hours she felt as if she had always been a part of it.

The head of the Department was on a buying trip to Europe, so she was told, and the words rang ominously in her ears. What exactly did 'buying art' in Europe mean? From the paintings displayed she did not have a high opinion of the man's artistic knowledge and, watching the Farrell clientele during the next few days, she reached the same conclusion about *them*! Pictures bought from Farrell's Art Department were obviously regarded as additional items of furniture.

'The drawing rooms of the upper middle class must have a pink and gold décor,' she said wryly to Jean Denton, the Assistant Manager of the Department, after she had sold her fifth view of Mont Blanc at sunset. 'I never knew people really bought things like this.'

'You're here to give the customers what *they* want, not what *you* want.'

'Does that mean we have to stand by and applaud bad taste?'

'You aren't applauding it. You're selling it. That's what business is all about—to sell.'

'Farrell's has a special reputation,' Samantha insisted. 'People all over the world know that we sell the best. The same way they know that Neiman Marcus in the States sells the most expensive!' She glanced round the walls and shuddered. 'No one could say these paintings are anything other than awful!'

'What about that?' Jean Denton pointed to a cluster of flower paintings—all derivative of the Dutch Masters.

'They're copies,' Samantha protested.

'We couldn't sell the real thing, Miss Byers. Paintings like that would run into tens of thousands of pounds, and the most expensive one we've sold here was for three thousand. After all, we aren't in competition with the West End galleries.'

'Of course we are,' Samantha argued. 'The only difference is that all the paintings *we* sell are rubbish!'

The woman went scarlet and Samantha was dismayed that her remark should be taken so personally. But the male voice that spoke behind Samantha suddenly gave the clue to Jean Denton's change of colour. It was not her vociferous criticism that had caused it but the fact that it had been overheard by Zachary Farrell. Quickly she swung round to greet him and the Assistant Manager tactfully disappeared.

'Miss Denton is correct in what she said to you, Miss Byers.'

How cold and deep his voice was, she thought. Cold and deep as an iceberg. The way the simile had come into her mind made her wonder if she was also describing her feelings about his character. After all, most of it was hidden and only to be guessed at, though there was little guessing required to know his present mood, if his lowered eyebrows and heavy scowl were anything to go by.

'We are not in competition with the art galleries,' he continued. 'They invest hundreds of thousands of pounds in their stock, whereas for us it's only a small part of what we carry.'

'Then why bother carrying it at all?'

'Because there's a demand for what we sell. Our clients wish to buy pictures for their home and we feel it our duty to supply them.'

'You would do just as well to give them coloured bits of wallpaper in rococo frames!'

'I'm sorry if our paintings aren't expensive enough for you,' he said frigidly.

'It has nothing to do with their value,' she flared. 'You can't be that ignorant!'

'We are not discussing my ignorance, Miss Byers, but yours. Until you know more about the way Farrell's is run—and why a Department supplies what it does—I suggest you make no further comment. My uncle asked you to work here for a year to learn the business. At the end of that time you might—and I even use that word without conviction—you *might* be in more of a position to give your opinion.'

'I don't need to work here for a year to know your Art Department is dreadful. I'm not an ignoramus on the subject. I have represented my mother for two years and——'

'Does being your mother's daughter qualify you as an expert?' he cut in.

'Two London galleries have asked me to buy for them,' she said stiffly. 'And they don't sell her work, so that wasn't the reason they made the offer.'

There was a slight pause before his shoulders lifted. 'I am sorry if I have misunderstood your experience in the art world, but I haven't misunderstood it in relation to our own Art Department. We run ours on quite different lines. As I said before, we are here to cater to our clients, not to educate them.'

'You could do both.'

'I am satisfied that we do one thing very well, without hankering for two. I would suggest that you cultivate the same attitude.'

He continued on his way and she watched him mutinously. His steps were soundless and his movements lithe. In his dark suit and with his jet black hair he reminded her of a panther: black and powerful and always ready to pounce. How long had he been listening before he had sprung out on her? Anger rose higher as she remembered his critical comments. So Farrell's gave their clients what they wanted? What he had really meant to say was that *he* gave the clients what they wanted, for in his own mind he was Farrell's. But one day he would learn otherwise. Larry was a part of Farrell's too. 'And so am I,' she thought darkly. 'Oh yes, Mr Zachary, so am I!'

When Samantha arrived at the Art Department the next morning there was a message for her to go to Zachary's office. With a heart that persisted in beating annoyingly fast, she ran up to the top floor, ignoring the lift which was too slow for her impatient mood. Breathless, she reached his secretary's desk.

'I believe Mr Farrell wishes to see me?'

'Not that I am aware of.' Mrs Fielding, who could have been the twin of Larry's secretary, looked suitably contrite. 'I am afraid the message was misunderstood. It was to ask you to telephone Mr Zachary's office. He has made arrangements for you to go to the Dress Department.'

'But I've only been in the Art Department two days. Are you sure there isn't some mistake? I was in Hardware for a fortnight and——'

'There is definitely no mistake, Miss Byers. Mr Zachary was quite clear about it last night. In fact I tried to phone you then, but you'd already left the store.'

'Why am I being moved?' Samantha asked bluntly.

'Mr Zachary felt you would be more at home in the Dress Department.' Mrs Fielding spoke without any change of tone.

'Will I be expected to put myself on the stand with the dummies?'

The greying head jerked up sharply, but the composed face gave nothing away. Were all secretaries to tycoons impervious to criticism about their bosses, Samantha wondered, or were they so used to it that they could ignore it?

'I'm just annoyed at being shifted,' she said hurriedly, knowing it was wrong to involve a stranger in a family matter. For this was a family matter. She was John Farrell's goddaughter and because of it had been placed in this position.

'I am sure you will enjoy working in the Dress Department,' Mrs Fielding stated. 'All the clothes there are exclusive to Farrell's.'

Smiling goodbye, Samantha went downstairs to tell the news to Jean Denton, who did not hide her relief that her assistant was being moved away from her with such speed. Feeling like a chastised schoolgirl, Samantha presented herself to Madame Vonet, a chic Frenchwoman under whose eagle eye the entire couture and ready-to-wear Department ran.

'You cannot wear your hair loose,' Madame said when the first greetings were over. 'And you are much too young. I like my assistants to be in their forties, particularly for couture.'

'Why?' Samantha asked.

'Because young girls cannot afford the prices of the clothes we sell here, and older women do not find it——' there was a tightening of the lined face—'do not find it heartening to be served by the young.'

'You mean because it reminds them of their own lost youth? I would have thought that the quicker a woman comes to terms with that, the better.'

'Please keep your opinions for the psychiatrist's consulting room, Miss Byers. I run this Department my way.'

'Mr Zachary Farrell sent me to work here,' Samantha said firmly, 'and you'll have to put up with me. I can put on a grey wig if you like.'

'A guard on your tongue would be better.'

Samantha could hardly wait for the day when Madame Vonet learned her true identity and, in the next couple of days of haranguing, almost blurted it out. Only her vow to remain incognito—which she had foolishly given to Zachary Farrell—enabled her to hold her tongue.

In the meantime the Frenchwoman seemed set on making Samantha's life a misery. Each day she had to change the clothes on the stands. It was a difficult task, for the dummies were made to Farrell's own design and were so lifelike that it was as complicated as dressing real people. Unfortunately Samantha did not have a good eye for size and she frequently dressed them in clothes that were either too large or too small, which necessitated taking them off again. The first time that she had dressed a dummy in a garment two sizes too large, she had skilfully pinned it at the back, only to be met with a shriek of fury when Madame's eagle eye spotted it.

'Stupid girl!' the Frenchwoman had hissed. 'Don't you know that if you put pins into chiffon it will damage the fabric? And if you spoil a garment the cost of it is docked from your salary?'

'I haven't damaged it.' Samantha had hastily withdrawn the pins, which immediately sent the dress flopping to the floor.

'Lift the skirt from the carpet!' Madame had wailed. 'It will pick up the dust.'

'No dust would dare settle in your Department, Madame,' Samantha had said solemnly, hoisting the garment on to her arm and at the same time lifting it over the dummy's head.

'Find a smaller size,' Madame had hissed.

'This is the smallest.'

'Then put another dress on the stand.'

'You told me to display this one.'

'Only because I thought it was the correct size for the model. Why don't you use your brain, Miss Byers? I assume you have one!'

Muttering angrily, Madame Vonet had stalked off and Samantha chose another dress to put on the model.

It was this same model which Samantha was dressing this morning, and it was now displaying an alarming tendency to lose its arms. She examined the figure with interest. It was extremely well-made, with a beautifully shaped torso and elegant legs. All the limbs—as well as the head—could be taken off, and she thought it would be amusing to switch the various parts around. Discarding such a frivolous thought, she re-fixed the arms into their slots and then stepped back to look at her handiwork. Darn it, she had got it wrong. The hands were pointing backwards. She giggled and stepped further away for another look, freezing into immobility as her body came up against a hard, immovable barrier and a cold hand placed itself on the side of her waist and pushed her firmly away. Face flaming, she turned and saw Zachary Farrell.

'I was—I was just looking at the dummy,' she stammered.

'Waiting for it to come to life and talk to you?'

'It won't do that,' she said solemnly. 'It's designed to be a Farrell woman—mute—the way you obviously like them.'

There was not a flicker in his pale eyes and the well-shaped mouth, with its full lower lip, tightened thinly. 'I suggest you dress it,' he said, pointing to the nude body.

'Is it giving you ideas?' she asked innocently.

This time he could not hide what he was feeling, though even then it was only shown by a swift indrawn breath, which he immediately released on a long-suffering sigh.

'You must have gone to a boarding school, Miss Byers. You have that particular juvenile sense of humour which they seem to inculcate.'

Giving him the pleasure of having the last word, Samantha turned back to the stand. But embarrassment had rattled her, making her movements clumsy, and though she tried to steady the model as she dressed it, she inadvertently pushed it. It teetered on the edge of its plinth and then, with a resounding crash, fell to the floor. The smiling head fell off and rolled ridiculously across the carpet to land at Zachary Farrell's feet.

Silently he stared down at it and then, still without a word, picked it up and held it out. 'Yours, I presume?'

'I bet you wish it was!'

'Full marks, Miss Byers,' he said softly and, placing it in her unresisting hands, walked away.

Her encounter with Zachary Farrell left Samantha shattered, and, long after he had departed, she thought of the many brilliantly cutting things she could have said to him had she thought of them at the time. Unfortunately he had a habit of rendering her speechless even before he said a word to her. It was his eyes, she decided. Those pale grey eyes. And his mouth too: the lips always compressed together as if he were afraid that by releasing them he would disclose their fullness and give himself away. That well-shaped, sensual mouth did not hide a man with a frigid nature. He might be cold and calculating in business, but with a woman he would be passionate and demanding.

'*Venez vite!*' Madame Vonet's sharp voice brought Samantha back to the present and she saw the buyer talking to a customer.

She was a narrow-faced young woman, petite and curvaceous, with dark eyes and shiny black hair that fitted her scalp like a satin cap. It was a supremely sophisticated style and threw into stark relief the bone structure of the face which, though not beautiful, was arresting. The forehead was slightly too high, the eyes a shade too close together and the mouth, if one analysed it, almost too full. Yet taken as a whole it was a fascinating face that one would never tire of watching. Samantha knew without question that the girl was foreign and found this confirmed when she heard her speaking in perfect French to Madame Vonet.

'The clothes you ordered have just come in,' the buyer was saying, 'but I have a couple of other dresses that I also think you will like.'

Madame turned to Samantha and briskly told her what to bring out from the stockroom. The dresses were all in the ready-to-wear range but were Italian and French and highly expensive, and she carried them into the salon and placed them carefully on a settee.

'Put them on a rail,' Madame hissed.

'There isn't one here,' Samantha protested.

'Well, get one from the stockroom.'

Annoyed that she had not thought of doing it herself, Samantha wheeled one out and soon half a dozen dresses were swaying delicately on the aluminium frame.

'Will that be all?' Samantha asked the buyer.

'Do you have better things to do?' the woman hissed.

'No, but . . .'

'Then stay where you are.'

Samantha did as she was told and watched as the customer disappeared into a fitting-room. Each time she put on another dress she came out to see herself in a mirror that would give her a more distant view. Only one of the outfits did not meet with her approval, and she nodded complacently at all the others to signify she was taking them.

A quick mental sum told Samantha that the bill would be in the region of [illegible] hundred pounds, and she swallowed hard when the girl reminded the buyer that she had said she had a couple of other garments to show her.

'A green suit and a white chiffon dress,' Madame

Vonet said. 'I'll fetch them for you myself.'

She disappeared and the girl sauntered over to a settee and sat down. An awareness of her body was apparent in every movement she made and Samantha was surprised to see that her hands, long and thin with brightly painted nails, were ringless.

'You are new here.' The words were spoken in English without any trace of an accent.

'It's my fourth day in this department.'

Feeling she had done her duty conversationally, the girl looked into the distance while Samantha, not sure whether to remain where she was, decided it was better to do so than to incur Madame Vonet's wrath.

The woman came out of the stockroom carrying a green suit in one hand and a white dress in the other.

'I'll try the suit first,' the girl said, and disappeared into the dressing-room.

Behind Madame Vonet the telephone rang and she nodded to Samantha to answer it. Samantha did so. The call was from Rome and the name of the caller sufficiently important to send her scurrying after the buyer.

'It's a personal call from Signor Petracci. Will you take it or shall I ask them to ring back?'

'Vittorio!' With an exclamation, Madame placed the clothes she was holding into Samantha's arms. 'Please attend to these. My call may take a little while.'

She hurried out and Samantha gave a half smile to the girl standing in a silken slip before the mirror.

'I don't have all day.' The girl ignored the smile and pointed to the suit.

Quickly Samantha unzipped the skirt and unbuttoned the jacket before passing them over.

The girl put them on, her impassive face brightening into vivacity as she looked at herself. 'Lovely. Green is my colour, don't you think?'

'Most strong colours would suit you,' Samantha replied. 'You have very dramatic colouring.'

'I suppose you notice it because you're so pale yourself.'

Samantha immediately felt insipid and wondered if the comment had been chosen with care or by accident. There was something about this client she did not like, though she was quick to admit her feeling could be caused by jealousy. After all, not many girls of her own age could buy so many expensive clothes without blinking at the cost.

'Yes, I'll definitely have the suit.'

She stepped out of it and dropped it carelessly on to the chair before swiftly plucking the chiffon dress out of Samantha's hands and slipping it over her head. There was a ripping sound and Samantha gave a cry.

'The zip! It isn't properly undone.'

'You should have seen that it was.' The girl spun round, giving Samantha a view of the back of the dress. Quickly Samantha lowered the zip. But the damage had been done and two inches of the delicate fabric had been torn away from the side.

'It's b-broken,' she stammered. 'I-I'll get a couple of pins and——'

'Don't bother. There's no point in my trying it on. I have no intention of taking anything that's been damaged.'

'You should have looked to see if the zip was undone.'

'What did you say?'

'I said you should have looked to see if the zip was undone. You don't just pick up a garment and put it on blindly.'

'Are you criticising me?'

Samantha swallowed. What on earth had made her get into this argument? Yet inevitably there would be one when Madame Vonet returned and it was as well to establish the truth now.

'I am merely saying I don't intend to take the blame for the dress being torn,' she said quietly. 'I didn't put it on you. You took it out of my hands yourself.'

'Before you gave me the suit,' the girl retorted, 'you unzipped the skirt and undid the jacket. I had every right to assume you would do the same with the dress.'

'I would have done if you had given me a chance. But you pulled it out of my hands.'

'I did no such thing!' With quick, angry motions the girl stepped into her own dress and whisked out of the dressing-room in time to meet the buyer, who was coming back in.

'Did you like them?' Madame inquired.

'I'll take the suit, but I can't take the dress. It's torn.'

'But that's impossible.'

'Not if you have a novice for an assistant.'

There followed a spate of excited French which Samantha could just follow, and which was clearly putting the blame on her.

'It wasn't my fault,' she cut in, and her interruption caused both women to stop in full spate.

'You will speak when you are spoken to, Miss Byers,' Madame said.

'I won't stand by and allow myself to be blamed for something I didn't do!'

Madame's bosom swelled with anger. 'Go into my office and wait for me there.'

Controlling herself with an effort, Samantha did so. What bad luck that something like this should happen to her today of all days. Madame Vonet swept in.

'And now, Miss Byers, we will get this little matter settled.' She was holding the offending dress and she bent to examine it, muttering audibly as she saw the extent of the tear. 'It will have to be invisibly mended. We won't be able to sell it as new.'

'But there's so much chiffon in the skirt. Once it's re-sewn——'

'Our clients do not expect to buy *seconds*,' Madame cut in, her whole demeanour one of horror. 'The dress will have to be marked down and put into our sale at the end of the season.'

'Surely not?' Samantha protested, dismayed at the thought.

'Are you telling me how to run my department, Miss Byers?'

'Of course not. But I do think it's unfair for a saleswoman to be blamed for something a customer did.'

'If Miss Bergérac tore the dress trying to get into it, it's your responsibility.'

'I don't see why.'

'If *you* aren't responsible for the clothes that are given to you,' Madame Vonet said sarcastically, 'then who is? The chimney sweep? Miss Bergerac is one of our most valued clients and I will not have her upset in any way.'

'I appreciate her value,' Samantha said. 'She must have spent over five hundred pounds this morning, but that still doesn't mean she isn't to blame for tearing the white chiffon.'

'*C'est fini*.' Madame gestured with her hands. 'The cost of repairing the dress will be docked from your salary. I imagine it will be about ten pounds.'

'As much as that?' Samantha's gasp was one of indignation, though Madame, thinking it one of dismay, lost some of her annoyance.

'Invisible mending is expensive. I am sorry, Miss Byers, but it will at least teach you to be more careful in future.'

'It might be cheaper for me to buy the dress for myself,' Samantha muttered, swiftly trying to calculate the discount price she would get.

'Do you normally spend two hundred pounds on a dress?' Madame sniffed.

'Occasionally I've worn dresses that have cost even more.'

Temper was beginning to fray the edges of Samantha's discretion. One of the perks of representing her mother was the fabulous clothes allowance it had given her. In order to get publicity for each art show, she had had to exert her charm on newspaper and television reporters, and an alluring appearance had been a great asset. But to say this to Madame Vonet was impossible and she suffered the buyer's look of disbelief.

'There is no shame in not being able to afford expensive clothes, Miss Byers,' the woman said. 'It is unnecessary to lie about it. I am sorry this unfortunate incident had to occur in your first week with us, but I hope it will teach you to be more careful in future with the clothes.'

'It will teach me to be more careful of Miss Bergerac,' Samantha said.

'Then that is a good thing too. She is a personal friend of Mr Zachary Farrell's.'

Madame Vonet swept out and Samantha followed more slowly. So that was Zachary Farrell's girl-friend! If only she had realised it at the time. Amusement superseded the anger she was still feeling at being unjustly blamed for the damaged dress. When she chose to have an argument with someone, she certainly took on the best! Still, Miss Bergerac was nowhere near the type she had imagined as appealing to Lord-High-and-Mighty. She had envisaged him with someone far more pliable and feminine.

'Don't stand there dreaming!' Madame hissed. 'Make sure the salon is tidy.'

Dutifully Samantha wandered around the pristine showroom, waiting for this ill-fated day to end. Because her mood was so despondent, she was more than usually delighted to see Larry coming towards her.

'My lunch date has cried off and I've come to see if you'll take pity on me.'

'It's the other way around,' she smiled. 'But can you wait twenty minutes? My lunch hour isn't due until one.'

'We can soon remedy that. Tell Madame Vonet you're going out with *me*.'

'I'd rather not. We have just had a bit of a row.'

'Then I'll tell her myself.'

'Please don't.'

Ignoring what she said, Larry strode over to Madame Vonet. There was a swift interchange of words and he returned to Samantha's side, followed by a pale-faced Frenchwoman who looked at her with something akin to fear.

'You should have told me who you were, Miss Byers,' she said in a thin voice. 'If I had known . . .'

'You would have acted differently,' Samantha finished for her. 'That's why I'm glad you didn't know. At least now I realise what your other assistants have to go through.'

'I don't generally take on assistants who have no experience.'

It was an admirable comeback and Samantha's half-smile gave the Frenchwoman full credit for it.

'Come on,' Larry intervened, catching hold of Samantha's arm. 'The commissionaire's getting a cab for me and I don't want to keep it waiting.'

CHAPTER FIVE

OVER lunch—which was at a nearby restaurant and did not involve taking a taxi—which had merely been Larry's diplomatic way of preventing a row, Samantha told him of the whole unfortunate episode.

'I wish I'd been a fly on the wall,' he chuckled. 'I would have loved to see you and Marie having a go at each other.'

'I'm not concerned with Miss Bergerac so much as the principle of the thing,' Samantha persisted. 'Why should a saleswoman be responsible for any damage a client does to a dress? I mean, a woman could step into it and tear the hem with her heel.'

'Our saleswomen aren't responsible for that sort of damage,' Larry said.

'They are—according to Madame Vonet.'

'The old girl was just being bitchy to you. She knows very well what the rules are. Any damage done to any article in Farrell's is paid for by Farrell's itself. Obviously if one of our staff goes on causing mayhem then we get rid of them. But in normal circumstances you wouldn't be expected to pay for any damage. I'll have a word with her.'

'Let me,' Samantha said, enjoying the prospect.

'Why not take the bill from her and send it to Zachary?' Larry suggested dryly.

'You mean he foots Miss Bergerac's bills?'

'We all do.'

She speared a scampi with her fork. 'You're being too subtle for me. You'll have to explain yourself.'

In a few words, he did. A year ago Zachary had instructed that everything Miss Bergerac bought at Farrell's should be charged to his own account, and since he, as Joint Managing Director of the company, was able to buy everything at actual cost, Farrell's did not even receive a minimum profit on the things Miss Bergerac bought.

'If she spent five hundred pounds in one morning,' Samantha murmured, 'she could spend a fortune in a year!'

'Six thousand pounds in the first year,' Larry murmured, 'and her second one is just beginning.'

It was impossible for Samantha to hide her astonishment. 'But that's a fortune!'

'Depends who's paying it.'

Samantha found this particular piece of information disagreeable and preferred to concentrate on the business aspect of it. 'You mean the store makes no profit on that six thousand?'

'Not a cent. It isn't very businesslike, I know, but then Farrell's don't make any profit on anything I buy here either. I'm Joint M.D. with Zachary, as you know.'

'How much do you spend here in a year?' The question popped out and Samantha immediately looked discomfited, though Larry seemed to find it funny.

'I don't mind you asking. After all, ten per cent of Farrell's is yours.'

'No, it isn't,' she said at once. 'I feel Uncle John gave it to me to hold in trust for you and your cousin. As soon as you have resolved your differences, I can give the shares back to you both.'

'I doubt if Zack and I will ever solve our differences. If you're waiting for that to happen, the shares will be yours for eternity! To get back to your original question, though. I know what you're getting at. Zack and I—and you too—should be allowed to buy from Farrell's at cost price. After all, if we owned a corner grocery shop, that's what would happen. And the fact that we happen to own a department store doesn't make any difference to the principle. But it should only apply to immediate family. If Marie was married to Zack it would be different.' He leaned forward. 'Why don't you bring it up at the next Board meeting? You know we're having one at the end of the week?'

'I didn't,' she said in surprise.

'Well, we are, and it would be a good time for you to air your views.'

'I couldn't. I would hate the first one of my criticisms to be something so—so personal to your cousin.'

'He scares you,' Larry stated.

'No, he doesn't. But you've got to admit it's a rather delicate issue to—to talk about a man footing his girl-friend's bills.'

'You aren't objecting to him footing them,' Larry commented, 'you're objecting to *us* footing them. Everything Marie gets here costs Farrell's both outlay and store space without a single penny profit in return. By rights, she should pay full price for everything. If one wanted to be magnanimous about it, then she should be treated like a senior member of the staff and get a decent-sized discount. After all,' he said, straight-faced, 'she does work hard at keeping our Managing Director happy!'

Again Samantha tried to ignore the personal undertones of the situation. It was hard to do, for the entire situation was caused by it. 'It would even be acceptable if she were given the same discount as the other directors.'

'Then say so at the meeting,' said Larry.

'What's wrong with *your* tongue? And why didn't you speak up ages ago?'

'What good would it have done? All Zachary needed

to do was to say "no". I couldn't force his hand. We both have equal rights in the company. That's why Uncle John brought *you* in.'

'What about when Uncle John was alive? Didn't he know about Miss Bergerac?'

'Sure he did. But he was too tired and drained to want to argue with Zachary. He let things slide.' Larry reached out for Samantha's hand. 'But he had enough determination to bring *you* into our lives. He knew that without someone to back me up, I'd never feel confident enough to take a stand against Zachary.'

'Couldn't Uncle John have left that ten per cent to one of the other directors? They know more about the business than I do.'

'They're also more prejudiced. No, Samantha, you were an ideal choice. You're honest, intelligent and incorruptible.'

Samantha was touched by this remark and liked Larry more at this moment than at any time since she had met him. He sensed her mood and took advantage of it by hailing a taxi for their short journey back to the store, kissing her swiftly but expertly before they drew up at the front entrance.

'Are you really going to go on with this nonsense of working your way through all of the Departments?' he said as he escorted her to the lift.

She nodded. 'Short of dividing my shares between you and Zachary, that's exactly what I'm going to do.'

'You could give them all to me,' he teased, and waved goodbye as the lift door closed.

His tone had been light, but she was sure his words weren't. Larry was as devious as Zachary but more subtle in showing it. She sighed and wished her godfather had not put her in this awkward predicament, or at least had talked to her about it when he had stayed with them in Ireland. If only she knew what he wanted her to do! Yet if he had known what to do himself he would not have given her a commanding vote in the event of his two nephews disagreeing on policy.

She reached the third floor and walked through Lingerie and Cosmetics to the Dress section. Madame Vonet had not returned from lunch and Samantha was glad of the opportunity of relaxing for a few minutes. Hearing about Marie Bergerac had ruffled her mood and she needed a chance to smooth herself down. The telephone rang in the buyer's office and she hurried to answer it, her hackles rising as she recognised the low, deep voice that came down the line.

'Zachary Farrell,' he said.

Deliberately she misunderstood him. 'You want the executives' floor, sir. You are on to the Dress Department.'

'I know I am. I also know I'm speaking to Miss Byers.'

'How clever of you to recognise my voice, Mr Farrell,' she cooed. 'Are you ringing to warn me that you're on your way down?'

'I'm ringing to remind you that while you are working your way round the company it will be best for our good name if you create as little disturbance as possible.'

'I beg your pardon?'

'It isn't my pardon you need, Miss Byers. It's Miss Bergerac's.'

'Are you suggesting I was rude to your girl-friend?' Samantha asked stormily.

'You were rude to a client,' he snapped. 'That's something Farrell's won't stand for.'

'I'm part of Farrell's too,' she snapped back. 'Ten per cent of it, Mr Zachary! You'd do well to remember it.' She banged down the receiver and glared at it as if it were Zachary Farrell's head. The bell rang again and she jumped back in fright, then caught her breath and picked up the receiver.

'We were cut off,' he said.

'No, we weren't, Mr Farrell. I put down the telephone, and I'll do it again if you talk to me the way you just did.'

There was silence for a few seconds.

'Look, Miss Byers,' his voice was so quiet she had to press the receiver hard to her ears to hear it, 'I've had a busy morning and I have a busy afternoon ahead of me. The one thing I do not relish is to be the centre of an argument between two irate females. Miss Bergerac was extremely upset at what happened this morning.'

'So she should be. Not content with getting her clothes free, she is also ruining the ones she doesn't take!'

This time it was the man who slammed down the telephone, and Samantha's astonishment gave way to amusement as she immediately dialled his office and asked to be put through to him.

'We were cut off,' she said sweetly as he came on the line.

'And we're being cut off again!' he said, and banged the phone down so loudly that it clanked in her ear.

Giggling, she worked her way through the rest of the afternoon, in such good humour that she could even take Madame Vonet's incivility in her stride.

But that evening, thinking over the events of the day, she was surprised by Zachary Farrell's telephone call. If he was foolish enough to listen to his girl-friend's account of what had happened at the store, he should also have been sufficiently businesslike to have heard her own account before judging her and finding her guilty. She was surprised he should behave so emotionally and saw it as a sign of his close involvement with the French girl.

'He's as stupid as all men when they are in love,' she said aloud, and immediately thought of Peter, who had never done what Jackie had wanted. Why did girls of Marie Bergerac's type—hard-faced little go-getters—always find things so much easier than genuine types like Jackie? She flipped idly through a glossy magazine to give herself something else to think about, and stopped as Marie Bergerac's pert face smiled out at her from above the collar of an exquisite chinchilla jacket.

'Mademoiselle Bergerac and Mr Zachary Farrell, attending the first night of Henri Bergerac's new play *Light of Day*.'

So the playwright Bergerac was Marie's father. Samantha pulled a face. At least the girl was not hard up for money, which made her behaviour with Zachary all the more extraordinary. Still, everyone had their own ideas of what constituted independence. And a good thing too, Samantha thought, for the world would be very dull if we were all alike. She stood up and, glimpsing her reflection in the mock Chippendale mirror above the mantelpiece, wondered what she would look like if her hair was black instead of honey-blonde.

The next morning brought Samantha a brief note from Mrs Elliott, Zachary's secretary, to say there was a Board meeting on Friday afternoon which she was expected to attend. On an impulse she rang Larry and told him she had decided to take up the question of what discounts should be allowed to Directors and their friends.

'Good,' he said. 'I'm glad you're accepting a woman's privilege.'

'What's that?'

'Changing her mind! I'll back you up, of course. That goes without saying.'

'Let's try not to make it personal,' she added. 'I don't want your cousin to think I'm getting at him.'

'It will be difficult for him not to think so, since he's the only unmarried director with a dependant!'

She laughed at his phraseology. 'I'm surprised *you* don't have a couple of dependants shopping at Farrell's.'

'I don't believe in letting my girl-friends get accustomed to the good life!'

'What happens when you take them out? I can't see you dining at a self-service!'

'It's different when I share things with them,' he chuckled. 'Which reminds me it's nearly a week since *we* shared an evening. How about having dinner with me?'

She agreed, more because she wanted to get off the line than because of a desire to spend much time with him. Larry was good company, but only—she had discovered to her surprise—when taken in infrequent doses. He was too light-weight intellectually for her to enjoy prolonged conversation with him, and the subject in which he was most interested—car racing—was one which left her completely cold.

On Friday she spent her lunch hour in Farrell's hairdressing salon. Obeying Madame Vonet's dictum that her saleswomen did not wear their hair loose, she had crimped hers into a bun, but now she asked for it to be re-styled and watched as several inches were cut.

'I don't want it short,' she protested.

'I'm only re-shaping,' the young man assured her, wielding his scissors demoniacally behind her.

'Hairdressers always say that and then leave you like a shorn lamb.'

'But such a beautiful lamb,' he said, snipping away merrily.

Defeated, Samantha subsided but, seeing the result an hour later, was delighted. The new style suited her exceptionally well. The shorter length enabled the back of her hair to curve into the nape of her neck and the sides, left slightly longer, lay softly upon her cheeks, swinging in a silvery cloud with each turn of her head.

'I look like one of those hair adverts on television,' she said happily.

'Better than that.' The hairdresser was succinct. 'Your colour is natural! I've never seen such a blonde before. Are you Scandinavian?'

'Just lucky,' she smiled, and gave him a handsome tip before returning to the Dress Department.

The previous day she had splashed out on a new outfit, but had deliberately bought it in a rival store, not wishing any of the directors she met today to see her in something that bore the unmistakable stamp of Farrell's.

'That's a charming dress, Miss Byers,' Madame Vonet commented as Samantha came out of one of the dressing-rooms wearing it. 'Pink is an excellent colour for you.'

'I don't usually go for blondes in pink,' Samantha confessed. 'It's a bit chocolate-boxy. But I thought this shade was rather subtle.'

'Because it has a tinge of blue to it that stops it from being too pink. And your brown accessories tone it down as well.' She eyed the high-heeled shoes and small flat bag. 'You are wearing a brown coat too?'

'I'm not bothering with the coat. The meeting is upstairs.'

Madame Vonet smiled graciously. 'I won't expect you back, Miss Byers. I am sure you will be tired.'

'If the meeting finishes in time, I *will* come back,' Samantha said. 'It's not that I'm a glutton for punishment, madame, but I'm keen to learn how this department is run.'

'Perhaps you would care to have lunch with me on Monday?' the buyer volunteered. 'I can fill you in on many things.'

Samantha duly accepted the olive branch.

'That's an excellent idea,' she said, pleased that peace had been established. Madame Vonet was good in her job and had to be seen in this context.

Smiling goodbye, Samantha went up to the top floor. All the executive offices were here, which seemed to her a remarkable waste of floor space in an incredibly expensive part of London. Surely the administration could be housed in suburban premises, leaving this floor to be used as a new department or an extension of one which was already too cramped—of which there were many. Was this what Zachary Farrell had in mind when he suggested expanding? She must find out more about his plans and why Larry opposed them.

Unwilling to enter his office on her own, she went in search of Larry. He was perched on the side of his desk, watching television. He lowered the sound as she came in, but the whine that still emanated from it told her he was watching a car race at Silverstone.

'You look good enough to eat,' he commented, eyeing her figure-fitting dress. 'I believe the apt description is slim as a wand.'

'What an original compliment, Larry. I hope you'll keep it just for me!'

'For no one else.' He went on surveying her. 'You've cut your hair.'

'How perceptive you are!'

'Beautiful young women merit attention, and you are more beautiful than most.' He sauntered over and placed his hands upon her shoulders. She had to tilt her head slightly to look at him when he was standing so close, and he lowered his own and kissed the top of her nose.

'See how well trained I am not to spoil your lipstick.'

'I'm sure your good training comes from practice!'

Smiling, he opened the door for her. 'You haven't

changed your mind about bringing up the subject of Marie, have you?' he asked as they walked along the corridor.

'I'm not discussing Miss Bergerac,' she said. 'I'm bringing up the whole question of discounts.'

He gave her a keen glance, but she ignored it and walked purposefully towards the Board Room.

Samantha had not been in it before and was impressed by its size, thinking again what a waste of space it was to have it here. Seated around a large oval table were ten men of various ages, though Zachary was the only one whom she knew, apart from Larry.

They all rose at her entrance, which made her feel terribly self-conscious, and she quickly took her place beside Larry while he affected a brief introduction. She remembered only a few of their names but knew that the company's accountant and lawyer were present, as well as the two financial advisers.

The meeting quickly got under way. Speeches were kept to a minimum, with Zachary rustling his papers impatiently if anyone digressed too far from the point under discussion. The subjects were diverse and ranged from re-apportionment of the monies to be spent on various departments—with increases being given to expanding ones like Do-It-Yourself, Domestic Equipment and Food—to new pension schemes for the staff, an extra number of security guards at night and a change in the lettering of the company's name. There was little disagreement about any of these issues. Only when it came to Zachary's announcement that he wished to double the size of the Food Hall at the expense of flowers and fruit did Samantha get her first chance to witness him in action.

'We can't cut down the fruit section,' one of the older directors said. 'We are noted for our first strawberries of the season; for the best guavas and paw-paws. It brings us good publicity too.'

'But it isn't bringing us new customers,' Zachary Farrell replied. 'And while we're on the subject I might add that I'm not only interested in getting new customers but in getting a new *type* of customer.'

'Why do we need a new type?' the banker asked. 'There are still plenty of rich ones to cater for.'

'There are many more in the middle range that I want to encourage. At the moment we are too esoteric in our policy. We're scaring away a large section of the community—the section where money is accumulating.'

'Now you're discussing the whole policy of Farrell's,' another director said, 'and that's something that will take a meeting in itself. In fact, several meetings,' he added. 'It isn't something we can do lightly, my boy. You know your uncle...'

'My uncle is dead,' Zachary said bluntly. 'When he left Larry and myself his shares he made no proviso as to how we should run the company. Had he done so I would have asked him not to leave me any shares. He knew that if I took over—if *we* took over—we would want to run things in our own way.'

'Zachary's right.' Larry spoke for the first time, and all eyes turned to him. 'I know my uncle didn't approve of some of the things Zachary wanted to do. You know what they are and we needn't go into them now. But one thing he did give both of us was *carte blanche* in the way we ran Farrell's once he was no longer here. We're only held back by lack of funds.'

'I'm glad you realise *that*.' The banker spoke in the dryest of voices.

'We do indeed,' said Larry with a charming smile in the man's direction. 'But we don't require any sizeable amount of money to expand the Food Hall. All it means is making two other departments smaller.'

'What other two departments?'

The argument waged back and forth and Samantha remained silent. She knew nothing about this side of the company, either the profit that came from selling food or how its value compared with any of the other departments, size for size. But if Zachary Farrell wanted it, she was sure it was a good proposition.

The thought surprised her and she analysed it while the men around her continued to talk, coming to the conclusion that though she did not like him, she intuitively respected his business acumen far more than she did Larry's.

'I think that's all on the agenda for today,' Zachary Farrell was speaking again. 'Unless anyone else has anything to say?'

'I have,' said Samantha in a clear but shaky voice.

All eyes turned on her and her cheeks bloomed to match the colour of her dress. She put up her hand to move away the soft wisp of hair that fell across her forehead and glanced at Larry as if for reassurance. His face remained impassive, but beneath the table his foot touched hers.

'I would like to talk about the discounts that are allowed to the directors. I appreciate that as one of those who hold voting shares I am in the privileged position—together with Mr Larry and Mr Zachary Farrell—of obtaining things at cost.'

'Members of the Farrell family always have everything at cost,' the banker said firmly. 'And we all believe they should continue to do so. It is a family firm and we are proud to keep it that way. The rest of us are perfectly happy with the forty per cent discount we get.'

'Oh lord,' Samantha thought. 'They think I want to give them more!' Colour bloomed more furiously in her cheeks and she was uncomfortably aware of pale grey eyes staring at her from the other end of the table, like twin points of silver light. If only she had not brought up the subject today! It was odds on that Zachary Farrell knew exactly what she was going to say. But it was too late to draw back and she had no recourse but to plunge on.

'I'm not suggesting we change the directors' discount,' she said in a breathless voice. 'But I think that the privileges the Farrells receive—mine included—should extend only to us.'

'But it does, my dear,' said the banker, paternalistically.

'That's what I wanted to establish.'

Samantha did not meet Zachary's eyes, but she had no need to, for they were piercing into her like probes.

'You have made your point, Miss Byers.' He raised his voice slightly to make it heard above the others. 'I suggest you discuss it more fully with my cousin and myself.'

Everyone at the table looked relieved and Samantha, not sure if she had won or lost the proposition she had put forward, rose uncertainly as the meeting came to an end.

Light refreshments were served—tea, coffee and delicious Farrell gateaux. Half an hour later everyone departed, leaving only the two cousins and herself.

'And now, Miss Byers,' Zachary Farrell said.

'Do call her Samantha,' Larry put in mildly.

His cousin ignored him and went on looking at Samantha with a dislike he did not bother to conceal. 'Let's get back to the suggestion you raised at the meeting. I assume you are referring to Miss Bergerac?'

'She was the person I had in mind,' Samantha said, and looked innocently at Larry, who shook his head and murmured, 'Not guilty,' in an expressionless voice.

'I don't consider myself guilty either,' Zachary said in a voice so deep it was almost a growl. 'The immediate family have always had this special concession. It applied to Larry's parents when they were alive and any other member of Uncle John's family.'

'Are you secretly married to Miss Bergerac, then?'

Zachary looked stunned at the question, as indeed he might, Samantha thought, for she was stunned by her temerity in asking it. What gave her the right to harangue him in this way? Larry and Zachary were Farrells. Between them they owned the store. But not quite. She had a small part of it, too. A small but highly important part—Uncle John's veto. That's what she was: his way of making sure neither of his nephews could overrule the other. And it was this that gave her the right to question anyone connected with Farrell's; be they the lowliest assistant or its most illustrious director.

'No, I am not married to Miss Bergerac.' Zachary was speaking again, though the effort it cost him was visible by the clenching of his hands and the pallor of his face. 'Is there anything else you wish to know?'

'Not for the moment,' she said composedly, and forced herself to look at him directly. 'While I can appreciate the benefit you obtain from Miss Bergerac's company, I don't think the rest of us obtain sufficient to warrant Farrell's receiving no profit whatever on an expenditure of some six thousands pounds per annum.'

'You little——' The rest of the words were bitten back, but his look spoke volumes.

Samantha held her ground and stared at him more defiantly, thinking of his earlier rudeness to her and the way he had sided with his girl-friend over the white dress.

'Samantha is right,' Larry said, as if knowing it was

time for him to speak. 'If you want to take care of Marie, that's your personal business, not Farrell's. Naturally she can have a discount on all future purchases, and we won't expect you to make up the loss on the past year.'

'I don't need your largesse,' Zachary said tersely. 'Work out how much you'd have got and I'll write you a cheque.'

'Or you could get married,' Larry added. 'Then Marie *would* qualify for things at cost!'

'Which might be too high a cost for *me* to pay,' Zachary replied. 'But you've made your point. In future I will pay for everything Marie takes.'

'There's no need to go the whole hog,' Larry protested. 'The other directors get forty per cent and so can she.'

Ignoring his cousin, Zachary Farrell looked at Samantha. 'Will that satisfy you, Miss Byers? Or do you wish me to pay the full cost on Miss Bergerac's purchases?'

'I'm quite happy with Larry's suggestion.' She hesitated. 'And while we're on the subject, I'd like to make it clear that I don't consider myself family and will not avail myself of——'

'Spare me the sacrifice,' he said roughly. 'You're part of our little triumvirate and needn't pretend otherwise. I can assure you I won't throw hysterics if your bills run into five figures.'

Before she could reply, he strode out and banged the door behind him. Dismayed, she resisted the urge to follow and apologise. He was angry and she could appreciate why. Yet she was not sorry for what she had said, only sorry that she had been forced into saying it. It had been stupid of him to put himself in such a vulnerable position.

'It's a pity he isn't married to Miss Bergerac,' she said

flatly. 'Then the whole thing would never have arisen.'

'Can you see him being happy with her?' Larry asked.

'I don't know either of them well enough.'

'You know Zachary. He's never any different from the way he is now—serious, bossy, single-minded.'

'Hasn't he any good qualities?' she asked with sudden irritability.

'He's great at sport and he's very patient.' The words came out without thought and Larry looked surprised at himself. 'Exceptionally patient,' he repeated. 'He was great to me when I was a kid. I'll go after him and have a drink with him. I'm sure he's got a bit of a sore head.'

'Don't talk about me behind my back,' she said as he went to the door.

'What makes you think I would?' He spun round to look at her.

'Two men together talking about an interfering newcomer,' she said dryly.

'That's not fair.' He returned to her side and pulled her close. 'I know I didn't have the guts to mention Marie myself, but I did back you up as I promised.'

'Yes, you did,' she said contritely. 'I'm sorry.'

'You should always kiss someone when you apologise.' He bent his head and touched his lips to her. His kiss was firm and she waited, half hoping to feel some emotion. But there was nothing.

'Samantha——' he breathed.

'Forgive me for interrupting.'

A deep voice drew them apart and she saw Zachary on the threshold. He ignored her completely and looked at Larry. 'Frank Goddard is waiting to see us.' He was referring to the banker. 'Have you forgotten?'

''Fraid so,' Larry said easily, not one whit embarrassed. 'I had more important things on my mind.'

Samantha's face flamed, for Larry made it sound as if

they had stayed deliberately behind in order to kiss.

'Do you want me to tell him you'll be along soon,' Zachary asked, 'or have you finished?'

'As a matter of fact, old chap, we've hardly begun!'

In normal circumstances Samantha would have laughed, but there was something about Zachary that made her feel uncomfortable. Again she wished that her first argument with him had not been of such a personal nature.

'Do go, Larry,' she said hurriedly, and went to the door. 'I'm going home anyway.'

'I'll pick you up at eight,' he said, and she knew he had spoken deliberately to acquaint his cousin with the fact, almost as if he was showing off his friendship with her.

'Fine,' she smiled, and walked down the corridor, leaving the two cousins alone and wishing, the way Larry had once done, that she too could be a fly on the wall.

CHAPTER SIX

SURPRISINGLY, Samantha had a thoroughly enjoyable weekend. She spent Friday evening and Sunday with Larry and went out on Saturday with Peter who, calling round to the flat to collect some of his records, had been sufficiently smitten with Samantha's looks to ask her out.

A weekend of masculine adulation did wonders for her ego, and on Monday morning she returned to Farrell's with a feeling of pleasure, quite forgetting Zachary's icy disdain of her. But she remembered it the instant she received a telephone call from his secretary, telling her, almost with a note of apology, that she should present herself at the Packing Department.

It required no appreciation of the way a store was run to know that the Packing Department was one sphere with which she had no need to concern herself.

'Are you sure there hasn't been some mistake?' Samantha asked, knowing full well there was not, and knowing also whom to blame for being moved.

'No, Miss Byers, there has been no mistake,' the secretary said. 'There was a note on my desk about it this morning.'

Hiding her anger, Samantha went to the basement where all goods to be delivered or posted were stored. There were only two girls employed on the actual packing—herself and another one—though there were a few others in the postal department. Luckily there was no heavy lifting to do and their time was spent mainly packing fragile articles and clothes which, though they were supposed to come down from the Dress Department ready for delivery, always had to be re-checked to make sure there was sufficient tissue paper between the folds and that the boxes fitted the garments as exactly as possible. No initiative was required and the work was tedious, particularly for Samantha who did not feel inclined to flirt with the cheery young messenger boys who whistled their way in and out. But her companion obviously delighted in her job and had been there for more than a year; sporting a minuscule solitaire diamond on her finger as proof of her success.

'My Bertie is in Shoes,' she said.

'That's better than going barefoot,' quipped Samantha, a remark which was met with a stony stare of incomprehension.

After a week of working in the basement which,

though air-conditioned, afforded her no view of the sky, Samantha was more than glad when the weekend arrived. On Saturday she went with Peter to the country. It meant refusing an invitation to go out with Larry, but she was glad of the excuse, for she did not wish him to commandeer her whole time. Peter was fun to be with and there was the added advantage of knowing he had no ulterior motive in wishing to be with her. Whereas with Larry she was not completely sure. Any guilt she might have had at going out with the man her friend loved was nullified by the knowledge that when he was with herself, he was unlikely to be falling in love with anyone else. To this end she chattered frequently about Jackie and what a marvellous time she was having in New Zealand.

Returning to Farrell's on Monday, she waited hopefully for a call from Mrs Fielding, directing her to another department. But none came and mutinously she went back to Packing.

If Zachary was waiting for her to complain to him, he would have a long wait indeed. She was prepared to stay down here for ever before she gave him the satisfaction of doing that. Still, even he would not be so ill-advised as to let this happen, since the whole purpose of her being here was to work her way through the entire store. Surely a week in Packaging was sufficient punishment for having had the temerity to criticise him?

The thought reminded her of Marie Bergerac and to her anger against Zachary she added astonishment that a man of such cold calculation should be enthralled by such a hard-faced little creature as the French girl.

Was it Marie's intelligence that attracted him? She had no way of knowing, for the girl had shown none towards her. Indeed, had she been intelligent, she would have behaved in a more civilised manner over the white dress. In which case, the events that followed would never have occurred.

By the middle of her second week in the basement Samantha was almost ready to go up and demand she be moved to another department. She knew she would have been quite within her rights to do so, but obstinacy still kept her where she was, though several of the parcels suffered at her angry hands.

'Mind how you wrap this one, Miss Byers.' The caution came from Jock, the senior man in charge, as he deposited a fragile Venetian bowl in front of her. 'You'd better pack it round with fibre-glass and cotton padding.'

Samantha admired the glowing colours of the bowl and wondered if it was going to be used for fruit or flowers or left to stand on its own as an example of beauty. Normally she did not like glass, preferring the robustness of ceramics, but this piece was exquisite enough to appeal to anyone with artistic taste. Carefully she placed it in the appropriate box and wedged it into position with padding. It was a priority delivery by hand, which meant she had to take it up to the commissionaire and wait at the entrance while he obtained a taxi. Sometimes this would be a lengthy business, for many drivers did not like delivering parcels, though usually the name of Farrell's was enough to get them to do so.

'Take it up as soon as it's ready,' Jock called across the room, and Samantha nodded. The movement sent a sharp pain across her eyes and she closed them briefly. Despite good ventilation she had had a headache for two days and knew it was caused by the fluorescent lighting to which she was unaccustomed, and the blaring of a transistor radio which her colleague kept beside her on the bench.

Making sure the address was clearly written on the lid, Samantha picked up the parcel and took it out of the department. Though the bowl was small, the bulky wadding made the package large and she was unable to see over the top of it as she carried it in front of her. She had to walk the length of a corridor before she came to the steps leading up to the Ground Floor, but she knew her way blindfold and she moved along at a brisk pace.

The suddenness with which she hit an immovable object took her by surprise. She side-stepped quickly, but it appeared the object was not immovable and did the same. This still left them barring each other's way and again she side-stepped. Once more whoever was on the other side of her followed suit.

'Do stand still,' she said crossly, 'unless you want the next dance!'

She raised the parcel high in the air and though this did not give her a view of the person blocking her way, it enabled her to see a pair of immaculately creased dark trousers and black shoes polished to perfection. Only one man would have shoes of such pristine brilliance, Samantha felt sure and, raising the parcel right above her head, she stared into Zachary Farrell's rigid features. The long nose seemed longer and the wide mouth wider, as it curved back in a sarcastic smile.

'Are you entering a weight-lifting contest?' he inquired.

'How else do you expect me to see?'

'Wouldn't it have been better to have put string all round it and carried it with the handle?'

It was an obvious thing to have done and she was furious for not realising it.

'I didn't think of it,' she admitted.

'That, I imagine, is a failing of yours.'

'I thought very carefully before I spoke at the meeting,' she came back at him, knowing what was in his mind.

His look was derisive. 'What makes you so sure I was thinking of the meeting?'

'Why else would you dislike me? You're annoyed with me for not letting your girl-friend walk all over me in the Dress Department, and you're angrier still because I——'

'Do you think it's only your behaviour with Marie that makes me dislike you?' he interrupted. 'Don't you know what your position here means to the running of Farrell's?'

'I know what it would mean if I wasn't here. If you and Larry were equal shareholders nothing would get done!'

'I don't happen to agree with you. My cousin is capable of assessing whether something is right or not, and in all the years we've worked together, we've always ended up in agreement.'

'Because your uncle was here to see that you did. But he obviously didn't think it would happen once he was dead. Believe me, Mr Farrell, I hate my position here as much as you do, and no matter what you think to the contrary, I knew nothing of Uncle John's intentions until after he had died.'

Because she was speaking with passionate conviction her voice rose. There was a ring of truth in it, as there was in the fearless look sparkling from her large grey eyes, and no man of sensibility could have denied it.

'If you're telling the truth,' he said grudgingly, 'I hope you will have the sense to vote with me over the annex.'

'I thought you'd shelved that idea for the moment?'

'Is that what Larry told you?' Zachary's voice was deep as a cello and she felt the throb of it in her body.

'He d-did mention it,' she stammered, hoping she had not given anything away.

'I wish I knew why he was against it,' Zachary said grimly. 'If we want to stay in business and compete with our rivals, we have no option but to expand. If we don't, we'll end up as a small, specialist type shop with a diminishing clientele.'

He straightened his shoulders, making her conscious of their width and the broadness of his chest. Because her present work meant her standing a great deal, she was wearing flat-heeled shoes, and it made him some inches taller than her. This may have been the reason why she suddenly had a heightened sense of his physical strength. It was odd that he had used the words 'weight-lifting' a moment ago, for that was exactly what she felt he could have done as a hobby. His biceps were hidden by his faultlessly cut suit, but their strength was evident, as were his large, well-shaped hands which, though they showed no sign of physical work, looked as if they could span her waist and break her in two. As if conscious of her eyes on them, his fingers twitched slightly, almost as if he longed to get them round her neck. The idea made her smile.

'I'm sorry if what I've said has amused you, Miss Byers,' he continued, 'but it happens to be important to Farrell's future.'

'I wasn't smiling at what you said but at—at the way we always fight when we meet. I wish you could realise that I also want what's best for Farrell's.'

'How can you know what's best when you're so inexperienced?'

'Intelligence can often compensate for experience,' she said sharply. 'That might not be the case where technical or scientific knowledge is required, but with something like a department store—or any type of business catering to people on a day-to-day basis—then understanding of human nature and some comprehension of the political and social scene is as important a factor as a minute knowledge of the ways a store is run. Sometimes, Mr Farrell,' she concluded, 'being too close to something and knowing too much about it blinds you to other considerations.'

For a half moment he regarded her. 'I appreciate your intelligence, but I would still prefer that you had actual knowledge. You're an emotional young woman and——'

'My head isn't turned by flattery,' she cut in swiftly. 'If I have to make a casting vote I would talk to the other directors before doing so.' She frowned. 'It seems so peculiar to have a Board of Directors and yet only allow three of them to control the company.'

'My cousin and I—and yourself—do not control the company. We only control the daily running of it. Any big change in policy requires money, and the Board as a whole have to give their approval before *that* is forthcoming.'

'But you still manage to get your own way, don't you?'

'That is my aim in life.' There was no humour in his face to soften this remark. 'My aims are often thwarted by lack of money, but I still regard myself and my cousin as the two people best qualified to make decisions. Farrell's has always been a family concern and should be controlled by the family.'

'You sound like a member of the Mafia!'

His full lip jutted forward. 'No doubt you think of me that way.'

The conversation seemed to be deteriorating and she knew that if she stayed here talking it would end up in another argument. Picking up the package and holding it in upraised arms—so that this time she could see where she was going—she started to mount the narrow flight of steps that led to a side entrance on the ground floor.

Whether it was self-consciousness at the belief that Zachary Farrell was still watching her, or because her upraised arms set her off balance, Samantha did not know, but she was halfway up when her foot slipped. In the normal course of events she would have gripped the railing to steady herself, but both hands were holding the parcel and she fell on to her knees. The steps were concrete and the sharp edge of one of them dug into her shin bone. With a gasp of pain she set the parcel in front of her. A red mist floated across her eyes and a wave of heat enveloped her. Almost at once firm hands were lifting her up and, though tears blurred her vision, she recognised the broad dark figure close to her.

'Are you hurt?'

'My leg,' she mumbled.

He bent towards it. His lids were lowered over his eyes, but when he raised them she saw silver sparks in the greyness.

'You've broken the skin. You had better go to First Aid.'

'But the parcel——'

'I'll deal with that.'

Shakily she rose.

'Can't you manage on your own?' he asked abruptly.

'Yes, thank you. But the parcel is an urgent delivery and——'

'Stop worrying about it! I said I would deal with it. Now do stop bleeding all over the corridor and go and see the nurse.'

Feeling foolish, Samantha limped to the service lift.

'The nurse is on the top floor,' he called after her. 'When you get out of the lift, take the first corridor on your left. She's in the room at the end.'

Samantha nodded and was glad when the lift doors closed her from his sight. Only then did she raise her leg to get a better look at it. There was a long jagged piece of broken skin and the area around it was already turning blue. It looked as painful as it felt and she was annoyed at how matter-of-fact Zachary Farrell had been about it. A shaky sigh escaped her. Considering they had been going at each other hammer and tongs only a moment before, it was foolish of her to expect him to show much sympathy. If it had been Marie Bergerac who had fallen up the steps...

Somehow she could not imagine the curvaceous French girl doing anything so ungainly and once again she was annoyed with herself for being so clumsy. There was something about Zachary that put her on edge.

'Nothing to worry about,' the nurse said after bathing her leg and putting a plaster on it. 'It will throb a bit, but it doesn't need any stitches.'

The telephone rang on her desk and she answered it, then held out the receiver.

'Mr Farrell,' she mouthed.

Wondering how Larry had got to hear she had hurt herself, Samantha said a surprised, 'Hello,' and was even more surprised to hear the deep voice that answered her.

'I've arranged for you to go home,' Zachary said. 'The commissionaire has a taxi waiting.'

'I'm not ill.'

'Just ill-tempered,' he rejoined, and put down the telephone before she could think of a suitable reply.

Driving home in a taxi a short while later, she mused on this latest example of Zachary Farrell's behaviour. It was the first gesture of friendliness he had shown towards her, which made her rather reluctantly admit that she had not displayed any to him either. Equally important, she had shown a predisposition for his cousin's company and, because of it, could not blame Zachary for believing she would side with Larry on any crucial point. She was always telling him she was unbiased, yet her behaviour belied her words. If she wanted to establish any friendship with the older Farrell cousin she would have to make her impartiality clearer. The best way of doing that was to see less of Larry; or to see more of Zachary. The very idea was laughable. He was totally occupied with Marie Bergerac. Recollecting his financial generosity, she was almost inclined to believe he was hopelessly enmeshed by the girl. Samantha's hair bounced as she shook her head. Zachary Farrell was too much in control of himself to be enmeshed by anyone. But if this was his character then he would never fall in love and his marriage—when he finally decided on it—would be a hard-headed decision. It was a saddening thought and she pushed it away from her. Zachary Farrell's private life was private and must remain so.

For the next ten days Samantha lived up to her determination to act impartially to both the Farrell men. Since she was barely on speaking terms with Zachary it put some strain on her relationship with Larry, and she was obliged to refuse his next three invitations to go out with him. Each time she found a different excuse, but she knew he was not fooled by it, and when he asked her for the fourth occasion, she could no longer find a valid reason for saying no.

'I was beginning to think there was something wrong with me,' he said plaintively as he drove her towards their favourite restaurant.

'You aren't the only fish in my little pond,' she teased.

'I wish I were. I'm crazy about you.'

'I'm crazy about me, too.'

'Can't you be serious, Samantha?'

'Not over you,' she said firmly. 'If you can't accept——'

'Okay,' he interrupted, 'I'll accept that fact. But temporarily only. One day I'll make you forget your neutrality.'

She refused to rise to the bait and instead asked him to tell her about the annual staff party which was being held at Zachary's home the following Saturday.

'It gives him a chance to play the king,' Larry shrugged. 'Welcoming the commoners to his home and all that.'

'I'm sure it would be far less bother for him if we had the party at a hotel in London.'

'Zack says the staff love to come to the country.'

'Maybe they do,' she replied. 'A day in someone's country home is less impersonal than an evening in a hotel.'

'Have you been talking to Zack about it?'

'Of course not. What makes you think I have?'

'Because those are the same words he used.'

Larry looked so disgruntled by what he had said that she tried to restore his humour in the only way she knew how. 'Will you be free to drive me down on the Saturday?' she asked.

If anything, this question made him more unhappy. 'Unfortunately not. Zack expects me to get there on Friday to help with the arrangements. It's a waste of time, actually—he has everything catered—but he does it deliberately to try and give me a sense of duty. He can't understand why I don't feel as paternalistic about Farrell's as he does.'

Samantha remained silent. Did Larry but know it, he was nudging her sympathies in Zachary's direction. It was a disquieting admission and she was afraid of it.

'Why don't you come down for the weekend with

me?' Larry broke into her thoughts. 'I'm sure Zack wouldn't mind.'

'I'm sure he would. I'll be happier just coming for the day. I'll try and get a lift from Madame Vonet. We've become quite friendly.'

'She has her eye on the main chance. She wants to expand her Department, and now she knows who you are...'

'I agree with all she wants to do,' Samantha said coolly. 'I've already told her so.'

'If you want my vote on it at the next meeting,' Larry said, 'just give me the word. You're so adorable I'll agree to anything you ask me.'

'Does the opposite apply, too?'

'Come again?' he asked, not understanding her.

'If you didn't find me adorable, would you disagree with what I asked you to do, even if it was a good idea?'

'What a nasty question! I refuse to answer it on the grounds that it would incriminate me!'

She smiled, but only with her lips. She was beginning to see why Zachary was uneasy at having her in such a key position. Any persuasive person could talk Larry into doing what they wanted—particularly if she was female and pretty—and if she herself were unscrupulous, she could get Larry to go along with any scheme she wanted. More than ever she failed to understand why Uncle John had not seen Larry's failings. Or had he been worried lest Zachary—left to himself—would become too much of a dictator?

'I'm not sure if I want to come to the party,' she said aloud. 'Zachary and I aren't friends and I'll feel uncomfortable in his home.'

'It was Uncle John's home before it was his,' Larry said. 'You used to like going there. Anyway, it will look odd if you don't come.'

'Why? None of the staff know who I really am apart from Madame Vonet.'

'They'll find out sooner or later.'

'How?'

'When you decide what you want to do with your shares. If you keep them, you'll have to take an active part in the company. And if you sell them, you're bound to hit the headlines.' His eyes narrowed. 'Do you know what those shares would be worth on the open market if you sold them?'

'They're not mine to sell,' she said promptly. 'I'm holding them in trust.'

'For whom?'

'Uncle John.' She saw his face fall, though he was quick to recover.

'You're an honest girl, Samantha. As honest as you're beautiful.' One hand lifted from the wheel and clasped hers. 'I shall expect to see you at Cramdene,' he said. 'If only to annoy Marie!'

'I hadn't realised she'd be there.' Samantha was dismayed at the prospect of seeing the French girl. 'Does she work?'

'Only at keeping Zachary happy.' Larry flung her an amused glance and, seeing her expression, thought better of what he had been about to say. His next remark was innocuous and for the rest of the evening they steered clear of anything to do with the store or the people who ran it. Only when he deposited her outside her front door did he again ask her to consider coming down for the weekend and, when she refused, gave her an overly warm goodnight kiss, as if to establish that whether she wanted it or not, he regarded her as more than a friend.

'I could go overboard for you,' he said huskily.

'You might drown.'

'What a lovely way to die!'

She was still smiling as she let herself into the hall. Larry deserved full marks for his exit line. What he lacked in strength of character he made up for in charm. It would be easy for a girl to lose her head over him. In a way it was a pity that she couldn't, for he would make an amusing companion. But she wanted more than a man who would amuse her. She wanted someone with strength and determination; a man she could not rule and one who would not want to rule her either.

That night she found it difficult to sleep and, rather than lie wakeful in bed, she went back into the living room and wrote a long letter to her mother.

'I wish I were back with you in Ireland,' she concluded. 'London life isn't for me. I find it too noisy, too smelly and too hectic. But the cousins still fascinate me and I'm treading a careful path between them. One day there's bound to be an almighty explosion between them and I'm doing my best to stave it off for as long as possible. But if Zachary tries to push ahead with his plan to build an annex, the eruption may come sooner than I want.'

She ceased writing and nursed her wrist for a moment, before continuing.

'You see, the other Directors are now willing to vote Zachary the money he needs for the building, but they can't do it if Larry votes against it—unless I side with Zachary, of course. It's frightening to think what power my small number of shares gives me.'

Once more she set down her pen, pondering as she had frequently done in the past weeks on why Larry should be so much against his cousin's wish to expand. It was unlike him to be cautious, particularly when he knew all the Board wished to go ahead.

'The time isn't ripe for us to get bigger,' he had said on the last occasion she had broached the subject to him.

He had gone on to give various reasons to substantiate his opinion, but she had not believed any of them. Yet neither had she been able to find any other, deeper reason he might have for trying to thwart his cousin. Yet if she sided with Zachary no one could thwart him. It was a power she wished she did not have.

She picked up her pen once more, but the impetus to write had gone and she closed the cap and set it on the pad. Yawning like a kitten, she went back to bed.

CHAPTER SEVEN

THE day of the garden party dawned perfect and, more than ever, Samantha longed for the soft green fields of Ireland and a sky that was rain-washed and clean. Here, the blue was always faintly tinged with exhaust fumes and no sharp breeze could clear the lead-polluted air. But once she and Madame Vonet neared Cramdene Lodge the atmosphere brightened considerably and, by the time they drove through the village of Cramdene itself, she could almost smell the sea.

Zachary's house was little changed from when she had last been there as a child, though there was no Uncle John coming down the side steps to greet her, and she had no desire to fling herself into the arms of the black-haired man who stood so calmly greeting the people who laughingly tumbled from the coaches and cars.

In casual sports clothes he still exuded the aura of a business executive, though he went out of his way to see that everyone had deck chairs on which to sit or knew where the pool was if they wished to bathe. Larry, equally casual in denim, joined Samantha some quarter of an hour after she had arrived, and apologised profusely for the delay.

'Zack insists I personally settle all the middle-aged females,' he grumbled. 'He'd have me sit with them all day, if he could.'

'An excellent idea,' she told him. 'You'd do wonders for their ego.'

'They'd do nothing for mine!' He eyed her lemon piqué dress with approval. 'You look like a lemon sorbet.'

'But no licking!' she giggled, and let him link his arm through hers as they wandered across the lawn.

'I hope you've brought your swimsuit?' he asked.

She shook her head. 'I didn't know there was a pool here.'

'Zachary only put it in a month ago. He's a great one for keeping fit.'

'I shouldn't think he gets much opportunity.'

'He walks to the office each day from Lowndes Square,' Larry told her.

'I didn't know he lived so near to me.'

'Don't get any ideas,' Larry teased. 'You wouldn't want to bump into Marie!'

Samantha felt a sense of shock. 'Does she live with him?'

'They don't actually share a home,' he said slowly.

The two people they were talking about came into sight. Marie was so petite that Zachary towered over her. It made him seem taller than he was, which no doubt made him feel good, Samantha thought sourly as she took in the highly expensive creation the French girl was wearing. And not from Farrell's either, she noted. As she watched them she saw Zachary's arm move. She did not know if it was deliberate, but the gesture loosened him from Marie's hold, and Samantha noted with satisfaction that the girl did not take his arm again.

'Sheath your claws,' Larry whispered.

'Were they noticeable?' Samantha asked.

'Only to me.'

'I don't like her,' she said defensively. 'That white dress still rankles with me.'

'Well, at least you don't have to serve her any more.'

'Nor pack parcels,' she responded. 'That cousin of yours kept me in Packaging for three weeks.'

'Zachary did?' Larry looked astonished. 'I'm sure he had nothing to do with it.'

'He was the one who sent me there,' she said spiritedly.

'You mean after the Board Room row?' At her nod he grinned. 'I'm sure once he did it, he forgot all about it.'

Samantha sniffed, not liking the thought that, having relegated her to the basement, he had put her so completely out of his mind that he had not remembered where she was.

'Anyway, I've moved now,' she said flatly. 'I'm in Millinery.'

'Let me know when you're in Bedding!'

'I didn't know you were a gardener.'

Larry roared with laughter. The sound caused Zachary to stop in his tracks and then come towards them. He had a smile on his face, which warned Samantha that some of the Farrell employees were watching them.

'I'm so glad you came—er—Samantha,' he said politely. 'You will join me at the Directors' table for lunch, won't you?'

'Nothing could keep me away—er—Zachary.' Her voice was demure, but she was delighted to see Marie Bergerac scowl. In bright sunshine the French girl's dramatic colouring made her look even harder. Despite her studiedly chosen garden-party dress of white lawn with embroidered marguerites, she did not fit into her rural surroundings. Yet she made Samantha feel young and gauche and intensely conscious of her fair hair blowing in the breeze, with a couple of ends wisping across her face. She put up her hand and pushed the curls away.

'Would you care for a swim?' Zachary asked.

This immediately made her feel she looked hot and dishevelled and she answered with unusual asperity, 'Not unless you don't mind nude bathing. I didn't bring a costume with me.'

'We have quite a few swimsuits lying round the house.' He turned to the girl at his side. 'You left a couple here, didn't you, the other weekend?'

'They wouldn't fit Miss Byers,' Marie said. 'She's skinnier than I am.'

It was such an obviously catty remark that Samantha almost miaowed. Hiding her amusement, she glanced quickly away from Marie's face and found herself looking at Zachary. He too had a gleam in his eyes and she was surprised by it. But yes, it was definitely there, and his next words to Marie proved it.

'Sometimes your English lets you down,' he said softly. 'The word you meant was slimmer.'

'Either way my swimsuits won't fit her.'

'Please don't be distressed about it,' Samantha said politely. 'I'll be perfectly happy to lie on a mattress and sunbathe.' Linking her arm through Larry's, she urged him away, not pausing until they were hidden from sight by a magnificent wall of scarlet and white rhododendrons.

'I love flowers,' she said, and touched a huge bloom with her hand.

'You're like a flower yourself.'

'A shaggy chrysanthemum,' she tensed. 'That's what Marie would say.'

'She's a bitch.' He moved closer, his breathing quickening.

Samantha sidestepped him and resumed walking, but this time back towards the house, unwilling to remain in a secluded part of the garden with him.

'I won't always let you run away from me,' he said behind her, and nipped her playfully.

She squealed and quickened her pace, turning a bend in the path so precipitously that she bumped into Zachary before she could come to a stop. His hands automatically clasped her waist to steady her. They felt warm through the thin cotton of her dress.

'No parcel this time,' he said.

'And no stairs for me to fall up either!'

A gleam showed in his eyes, but it faded as Larry came into sight. Dropping his hands to his sides, he moved away, following the path they had just taken.

Buffet lunch—prepared by Farrell's own catering department—was served on the lawn. Small tables had been set up, each with its bottles of wine and fruit drinks. The formality of the first hour had gone and people laughed and joked and wandered from one table to another, though none ventured to the large round one where Samantha sat with Zachary and Larry and the other Directors.

'This isn't very democratic,' she commented, half to herself, half to anyone who was listening.

'You think each of us should be sitting at one or other of the tables?' It was Zachary who took up her remark.

'Don't you?'

'No. We tried it one year and it was like a blight on the whole party.' He glanced over his shoulder at the noisy crowd. 'The staff like to know we're giving a party for them—it makes them feel on equal terms with us—but the moment we get too close, the equality disappears and we're "Mr Zachary" and "Mr Larry" again. It's much better if we keep our distance.'

'I hadn't thought of it that way.'

His tone lowered. 'As I said once before, you rarely do think before you speak.'

She coloured. 'And you always do?'

'It's safer.'

'Do you always play for safety?'

'It's a foolish man who gambles when there's no need.'

'Have you never taken a chance?'

'Are you asking me or tempting me?'

His stare was so intent that she quickly lowered her eyes to her plate, spooning up her ice-cream with a relish she did not feel.

'Would you care for some more?' he asked agreeably.

'No, thanks. I've had quite enough.'

His smile was sudden and surprising, showing strong white teeth. He was handsome, she thought involuntarily. How odd that she had not noticed it before. But then she had never seen him smile before. Until now, he had always scowled at her.

'My offer of more ice-cream was a genuine one,' he said. 'You looked as if you were enjoying it.'

'You didn't enjoy yours.' She pointed to his plate, where the ice-cream had already melted.

'I haven't got a sweet tooth.'

Her mouth opened and closed and his eyes gleamed. 'I'm glad you thought better of that, Samantha.'

'How did you know what I was going to say?'

'On your past record I'm sure it wasn't going to be something complimentary!'

She half looked away from him. He would be surprised if he knew she hadn't intended to be rude. 'It's too nice a day to quarrel, don't you think?'

'If you say so.'

'Then let's bury the hatchet.'

'Not in my head, I hope!'

'Don't tempt me or I might forget my good intentions!'

'I'm not frightened of you, Samantha. Place the hatchet where you will.'

He bent his head forward and she stared at his thick black hair, shiny and well kept. His neck was well muscled and there was a whiter line of skin where his collar pulled away from it. She half raised her hand to touch it and then drew it back, glad he had not seen the gesture.

'Have you dropped something, Zachary?' Larry asked.

'Samantha dropped her knife,' said Zachary, straightening and regarding her without the vestige of a smile before turning to Marie, who was on his other side.

After lunch, everyone was free to do as they liked. Some played tennis on the hard court that lay on the east side of the house, others continued to swim, while many preferred to stroll on the lawns, enjoying the sunshine. Tea and cakes were served at four and then a quartet of young musicians began to play in one corner, where a floor had been set up. Immediately a crowd gathered and started to dance and Larry regretfully left Samantha in order to do his duty on the floor. Samantha, seeing Fred from Packing bearing down on her, skilfully darted behind some bushes. She would not be able to remain hidden here for long and, still using the shrubs as a barrier, retreated along them until she reached the house.

At once she felt the past closing in on her. The hall was furnished in exactly the way she had remembered it, and there was still the same atmosphere of quiet luxury which she had always associated with this house.

The furniture was in the best English tradition and there were fine Constable paintings and Turner watercolours on the walls. She would have liked to wander around the downstairs rooms and revive old memories but, telling herself that it was now Zachary's house and she had no right to do it, she went across the hall to the glass door at the other end, expecting it to lead her into another part of the garden.

Instead she found herself in a square patio she had never seen before. It was Portuguese in atmosphere, with a gaily tiled floor and a white, wrought-iron table and chairs set in one corner. A growth of vines sprouted up one wall and along some overhead poles, while against the south wall a peach tree flourished. Further along this wall, half hidden by a mass of leaves, she saw a narrow wooden door and, thinking it would bring her into the garden, she opened it.

Her surprise this time was much stronger, for she found herself in a workroom. Curiosity kept her there and she moved in for a better look at it. Everything was clean and tidy; even the sawdust on the floor was in a neat pile. Tools were clipped on a large square of peg-board and expensive electrical equipment—far more elaborate than the usual handyman's do-it-yourself gear—was ranged on a workmanlike bench. She bent to examine one elaborate metal machine but could not make out its function. As she straightened she saw that a table was in the process of being made. The base was on the floor, but the top was almost in front of her. It was circular and some two feet in diameter and was a superb example of elaborate marquetry. Beside it lay a pencil sketch showing what the table would be like when it was finished. She bent again to touch its surface, her fingers carefully exploring the wood. What an intricate pattern of different veneers there were! This was truly a labour of love.

There was a sound behind her and she turned guiltily, tensing as she saw Zachary.

'I came in here by accident.' Her voice sounded nervous and she took a deep breath. 'I was looking for a quieter part of the garden.'

'I thought you would be enjoying yourself dancing.'

'Not with flat-footed Fred.' He looked blank and she explained: 'An old friend of mine from Packaging. He hasn't seen me since I moved from the department and I didn't like the gleam in his eye.'

'I take it you aren't hankering to return to Packaging?' Zachary said gravely.

'I think you can safely say that!' Not wishing to talk about Farrell's, she waved her arms around her. 'This is a marvellous workshop. Does it belong to one of your men?'

'It's mine.'

She was staggered. 'You don't mean you made this?' She pointed to the table and he nodded and came over to stand beside it. He put his hand on the top and she saw how well-shaped the fingers were, the nails immaculate and cut short. The extension of his arm pulled back the cuff of his shirt to disclose a fine sprinkling of hairs on his wrist. Quickly she looked at the table.

'I can't believe you do all this work.'

'I promise you I do. It's my hobby.'

'It's a very unusual one.'

'I find it relaxing.' He rubbed the surface of the table. 'Cutting all the different woods, putting in the minute pieces and making sure they don't break, stops me from thinking of anything else.'

'It still sounds like hard work to me.'

'It's a different kind of work. Wood doesn't answer

back and if it's wrong, I can always re-do it.'

'Have you made any other things?' she asked.

'A nest of tables and a spinet.'

'I'd love to see them.'

'I'll show you.'

She was touched by his eagerness. He was like a little boy showing off his toys. She followed him back into the house and across the hall to a room that was obviously a small sitting-room where he spent a great deal of time, for there were magazines and papers left haphazardly on the table in front of the chesterfield. The spinet stood in the corner and she gave an exclamation of pleasure as she saw it.

'It's beautiful.' She bent to examine it carefully. 'It's a genuine antique.'

'The top isn't. It took me six months to make it.'

'I can believe it. You've used the most unusual woods.'

'Ten different kinds. In the table I've nearly finished, there are fifteen varieties.'

'How long have you been working on that?' she asked.

'Six months. But it's almost done.'

'Just a bit more nailing and screwing!'

He shuddered. 'I can see you don't know how antiques are made.'

She giggled. 'You can't make an antique. It either is, or it isn't.'

'I'm making it the way antiques *were* made.' His smile was slight but genuine. 'You can't find a nail or a screw in anything I've done. It's all tongue and grooved.'

'Oh dear,' she said plaintively. 'I always seem to say the wrong thing to you.'

'But rather charmingly this time.'

Her head turned quickly towards him and her blonde

hair swung forward. 'That's the first compliment you've paid me, Zachary.'

'I've thought of several before now.'

'I would never have guessed.' She smiled. 'The last few times we've met, you've looked as though you wanted to bite me!'

His eyes glittered. 'That could be a compliment too.'

Her lids lowered and she felt him move towards her.

'So that's where the two of you are hiding?'

Marie's voice shattered the delicate atmosphere and Samantha backed towards the fireplace as the girl, followed closely by Larry, came in.

'The coaches are leaving, Zachary,' he said. 'Time for us to go and wave goodbye.'

'I must be off too,' Samantha murmured. 'Madame Vonet will be waiting for me.'

'Don't be silly,' Larry put up a hand to stop her. 'I'll drive you back later. I've made arrangements for us to have dinner here.'

Her heart began to beat quickly and she glanced at Zachary.

'By all means stay, Samantha,' he said quietly.

'That will be lovely.' She felt irrationally pleased at the prospect.

'What time are *we* going to town, darling?' Marie asked, sinking into an armchair.

'As soon as the coaches have gone,' Zachary replied. 'We don't have to be in town before eight.'

'I shall have to go home and change first.'

'That shouldn't take you more than an hour,' he teased.

'You know you'll never give me as long as that. You'll be pounding on the bathroom door after ten minutes.'

Samantha tried not to hear what was being said. She also tried to close her mind to the disappointment she felt at discovering Zachary was not going to be here. She was behaving ridiculously. It would be much more relaxing to be alone with Larry than to make stilted conversation with Zachary and Marie. Yet a moment ago she had not been at all stilted with him. From beneath the fan of her lashes she watched him. He seemed oblivious of her presence and was concentrating entirely on the girl sitting in front of him. All at once he went to the door.

'Come on, Larry,' he called, 'you're a Farrell too!'

Muttering good-naturedly, Larry followed him out. Samantha wanted to follow but knew it would be too pointed if she did. With an effort she sat down and tried to look nonchalant.

'It was naughty of you not to tell me who you were when we first met,' Marie drawled.

'I'm working my way through Farrell's to find out what it feels like to be employed there,' Samantha said. 'At least now I've some idea what a vendeuse has to go through with different customers.'

The smile on Marie's face was stiff. 'You don't mince words, do you?'

'I see no point. No matter what I say to you, you'll tell Zachary something different.'

'You're angry with me?'

'I was,' Samantha admitted. 'I'm not any more.'

There was the sound of a revving motor and Marie turned her head. 'The first coach has gone,' she said with satisfaction. 'Thank goodness it will soon be over. These parties are such a bore.'

'Why did you bother coming, then?'

'Because Zachary expected it.'

'I hope he appreciates the sacrifice you've made!'

'I'm sure he does,' Marie said, and uncurling herself from the chair, went out.

Morosely Samantha wandered round the room. Was it too late to tell Larry she had changed her mind and wanted to go back to London? But even if she did, he would still expect her to have dinner with him. It would look too obvious if she tried to pretend she had forgotten she had had another engagement.

'That's over for another year,' Larry said behind her, and she felt his hand on her shoulder as he pulled her back to rest against him. 'I'm glad we're staying behind,' he murmured into her ear. 'Do you know, this is the first time I've got you in my home?'

'It's Zachary's home,' she corrected.

'I still think of it as mine,' he said easily. 'Anyway, what I meant was that we aren't in a restaurant with people looking at us.'

'You love being looked at by all the women,' she said lightly, pulling away from him.

'There's only one woman I want to look at me,' he said. 'And that's you.'

Samantha wished she had not agreed to stay here. More than ever she had a presentiment of fear about the evening ahead.

Zachary and Marie left for London soon after the last departing coach, and Samantha's uneasiness grew at finding herself alone with Larry in a country house miles from London. True, there were servants around, but they were all well trained and did their job and then disappeared out of sight and—worse still—out of earshot. The knowledge was disquieting.

'Care for a stroll before it gets too cold?' Larry asked.

She shook her head and settled herself in an armchair by the enormous windows that overlooked the now peaceful garden. Apart from some overturned chairs in the distance, it was difficult to believe that a short while ago the lawns had been teeming with people.

'I don't know how you could give up your share of this,' she said. 'It's so beautiful and peaceful here.'

'Country living isn't my scene.'

'You once said you weren't the town type either.'

'I'm not,' he agreed. 'I prefer the sporting life.'

'Racing cars,' she smiled, remembering his hobby. 'You surely don't take that seriously?'

'I take it very seriously. Cars aren't just a passing interest with me. And there's more to racing than going round and round a circuit. It's the only real way of testing a car; of finding out how to improve it and if the new ideas you've put into it will work.'

'Like special tyres and new kinds of brakes or suspension?'

'Something like that.' He hesitated momentarily before saying: 'I'm working on a way of cutting down petrol consumption. All the tests I've done so far show that it works.'

'That's fabulous. Have you taken it to a car manufacturer?'

'It would be a waste of time. They'd turn it down.'

'Why?'

'Because it would mean re-tooling and that would cost them a fortune.'

'Then how do you hope to sell it?' she queried.

'By putting it into a car of my own design.'

'That would cost a fortune too.'

Again he hesitated, but this time decided not to pursue the subject and, when he spoke, it was to ask if she wanted a wash before dinner. She accepted the offer and he led her upstairs to a bedroom. The house was not as large as it looked from the outside and had a homely quality about it which she had not remembered. But she had visited it when she was a child and had been overawed by its grandeur. Today she saw it with the eyes of an adult and recognised it as a well-loved and well-lived-in country home. It was hard to see Zachary in this setting until she recollected the workshop and the beautiful rosewood table top. A man with the patience to do such intricate work would also enjoy the peace of the countryside.

When she went downstairs to the drawing-room Larry was waiting for her with a drink. Holding it in her hand, she wandered over to the window again. The summer day was ending and the blue sky had turned to purple, softening the horizon and blurring the outlines of the trees.

'It's beautiful,' she whispered.

'So are you,' Larry said softly. 'I never realised until I saw you here, how beautiful you were.'

The depth in his voice made her feel uncomfortable. She did not wish to arouse such emotion in him. With a shrug she continued to sip her drink.

'Beautiful but cool as an ice maiden,' he went on, coming to stand beside her. 'It's that long fair hair of yours, darling. Do you remember the story of Rapunzel?' His hands were warm on her shoulders. 'The Princess let down her long fair hair and the Prince climbed up it to her bedroom.'

'He climbed up her hair in order to get into the castle and rescue her,' Samantha corrected. 'Anyway, my hair is short.'

'Spoilsport!' he chuckled, and pulled her back until her body was resting against his.

She felt his heart beating fast and tried to appear unconcerned. 'Can we go away from the window, Larry? It's getting chilly.'

'Little liar,' he teased, and led her further back into the drawing-room. 'Do you know this is the first time I've been alone with you since I met you? Until now we've always been surrounded by people.'

'The servants are here,' she said abruptly.

'Too far away to hear us.'

'You make that sound ominous.'

'And you make it sound as if you're afraid of me. Are you, Samantha?'

'I will be, if you go on looking at me as if you're getting ready to pounce!'

He laughed and settled himself in the corner of the settee. Samantha relaxed too, glad she had managed to change the mood and hoping she would be as successful the next time Larry had the inclination to wax serious. She had professed not to be nervous with him, but she had been lying. For all she knew, the servants could have been told to go after they had served dinner, and she would then be entirely alone with Larry.

Dusk gave way to darkness and Larry lit the candles on the small table where a cold supper had been set for them: asparagus vinaigrette, fresh salmon and cucumber salad and a bowl of strawberries and cream. There was champagne on ice in a silver bucket and a silver thermos of coffee was set on the sideboard. It was an ideal supper to partake of with the right man, she thought, and knew with certainty that Larry was not the one. But would the right one ever come along? An image came into her mind—too blurred to be distinct—and she shook her head and pushed it away.

'If I had met you earlier,' Larry said softly, 'I don't think I'd have sold my share in the house to Zachary.'

'It's just as well you did. I can't see him giving up his share to *you*.'

'He offered to do it.'

She hid her surprise at his being so accommodating. 'Where would he have gone?'

'He would have found another place. Zachary's a resourceful chap, you know.'

She could believe it, but did not say so, unwilling to talk about Zachary for reasons she could not define.

Supper over, they returned to the drawing-room for coffee. Larry turned on the tape deck and a Haydn symphony infiltrated into all four corners. With an exclamation Larry turned it off.

'Not my cup of tea,' he said, and inserted a fresh cassette.

The liquid notes of Ella Fitzgerald took over and Samantha sighed, infinitely preferring to have heard the Haydn at this particular moment. Had Zachary been here she knew he would have preferred it too. Yet how did she know? She pondered on the question and decided it could only be due to intuition. Yet intuition also told her that a man who spent his leisure designing and making intricate and beautiful furniture could not find pleasure with such an obvious woman as Marie Bergerac. However, in this case intuition was wrong. Zachary not only found pleasure with Marie, but sufficient of it to keep him enthralled for two years. It was a chastening thought to acknowledge that a man, for all his far-seeing sharpness in business, could have fallen foul of an alluring body and provocative face.

With a start she felt Larry's arm come around her. He pulled her back against him and placed his cheek on hers. His breath smelt of whisky and wine, reminding her that though she had drunk sparingly, he had not done the same. Fear trembled through her and he took it for a different kind of emotion and ran his lips along her cheek.

'Relax, Samantha. No one will come in and disturb us. Kiss me, sweetheart.'

'It's late. We should be leaving.'

'What's the hurry?'

'We've a long drive back.'

'Then why bother to go?' His lips found the corner of her mouth. 'There's no reason for us to rush back. We can stay here tonight and have the whole day here tomorrow.'

'I'm going out tomorrow.'

'I don't believe you.'

'It's true.' She tried to pull away from him, but his grip tightened. Sensing that it would be wrong to try a show of strength with him, she again forced herself to relax. 'It's been a lovely evening, Larry, but I really do have to get back to town.'

'Kiss me first. You're so cool, Samantha, so untouched.'

As if fired by his own words, his fingers dug painfully into her back as he pressed her down upon the settee and leaned his body heavily on hers. It was impossible to avoid his kiss. She tried not to be sickened by the moistness of his mouth and his heavy breathing. She did not want Larry to hold her and touch her, and most of all she did not want him to kiss her.

'Relax,' he whispered, and moved his hands lightly over her breasts.

'Larry, don't!' She caught hold of his arm and held it still.

'Why not?' he pleaded. 'You don't need to be scared of me, Samantha.'

'I'm not.'

'Are you scared of yourself?'

The conceit of the remark almost made her laugh, but she stopped herself in time. Larry had a sense of humour, but it was not strong enough to enable him to laugh at himself.

'Yes,' she lied. 'You're so handsome and strong that . . .'

She let the rest of her words trail away, holding back an urge to kick him as she heard him give a sigh of satisfaction.

'I wouldn't do anything to hurt you, angel. I only want to love you. To make you happy.' As he spoke he started to lower the zip of her dress. His movements were as expert as his caressing voice, but she was equally expert in avoidance and she wriggled free of him and stood up.

'I really must be getting back to town, Larry. If you want to stay the night, I'm sure I can get a train.'

'Don't be silly! If you're determined to go I'll drive you back. There's no fun in staying here by myself.' He rose and came towards her. 'Why not change your mind and stay?'

'I haven't any change of clothes with me.'

'You don't need anything.' His arms came round her and his lids lowered over slumbrous eyes. 'I'll keep you warm.'

'Not warm enough,' she said lightly.

'Try me.'

'Another time.'

He sighed. 'What a difficult girl you are to please! But I'm not the type to give up easily, so be warned.'

'I'll bear it in mind.' Still keeping her voice light, she pushed him towards the door.

Not until they were in the car and heading north did Samantha breathe a sigh of relief. In future nothing would induce her to be alone with Larry. In a restaurant or theatre he was manageable, but when no one was within call he could become hard to handle. The car slowed down and the sound of the engine died as Larry brought the car to a halt in a lay-by.

'What's wrong?' she asked, keeping her voice cool.

'Nothing.' He moved across the space between them

and pinioned her against the door. 'You can't escape from me here, my angel. You're mine now. All mine.' His hands were heavy on her, but she was still determined not to show any fear.

'Don't be silly, Larry. It's late. Let's get back to town.'

'Why all the rush? If you do have a date with someone else, it isn't until tomorrow, and that's hours away. We've got all the time in the world.'

'It's cold in the car.' She pressed her hands against his chest. 'You can come up to the flat when we get back. It will be more comfortable there.'

'We can be just as comfortable here.' He half turned and pressed a knob on the dashboard. The entire front seat rolled down and Samantha went down with it, caught off-balance by the unexpected movement. Before she could struggle up into a sitting position, Larry was on top of her, his breath hot against her neck. She went on struggling to rise, but his weight prevented her, and though she tried to slide out from underneath him, he prevented this too by moving his legs and blocking her body.

'Please,' she said urgently.

'You needn't say please,' he said huskily, 'I'm only too willing.'

'That wasn't what I meant.' She pushed against him. 'Larry, don't be silly! You're hurting me.'

'Then stop struggling.'

'Then let me go.'

'No. I want you, Samantha. I don't know how I've kept my hands off you all day. Stop pretending you don't feel the same about me. Let yourself go.' He rained kisses upon her face and throat and along the curve of her breasts.

Goose pimples rose on her skin and she suppressed a shudder of loathing. 'Let me go, Larry!'

'Kiss me,' he said, ignoring her plea and roughly cupping her chin. 'Kiss me.'

She tried to resist him, but his hold was too strong and she was powerless to move as his head came down. She clenched her teeth and he shifted himself and rested more heavily on her. 'Kiss me,' he commanded. 'Don't be so frigid.'

With a strength she had not known she possessed, she gave him a violent shove. He slipped on to his side and with a quick wrench she slid forward on the seat and reached for the door handle. Miraculously her hand found it at the first attempt. It turned beneath her grasp and the door swung open so that she half fell out on to the ground. Not waiting to straighten properly, she scrambled away from the car, only standing upright when she reached the bonnet.

'Samantha!' Larry called. 'Come back!'

Ignoring him, she ran headlong down the road. His steps sounded behind her and she ran faster. The road was lit by moonlight and, had there not been a bend in it, she would never have escaped him. But it curved sharply to the left and as she raced round the corner she saw a gap in the hedge. Without thinking what might be on the other side, she dived through and crouched down on the earth, her heart beating so fast with fear that she almost did not hear his steps running past. But his voice was loud in her ears, calling her name and commanding her to stop.

'Samantha, don't be a fool! You can't get away from me. Come back and I'll drive you home.'

She crouched lower still, praying he did not see the gap in the hedge and come to investigate it. His steps were almost upon her, the soles of his shoes crunching the pebbles on the verge.

'You must be here somewhere,' he muttered, and then

raised his voice. 'I'll wait for you in the car. Stop acting like a fool and come back.'

His footsteps receded and there was the slamming of a door and then silence.

Slowly Samantha moved her cramped limbs and quietly raised herself. Though Larry had returned to the car and was out of sight, she would have to move quietly in order for him not to hear her. Keeping in the shadow of the hedge where her steps would make no sound on the soft earth, she began to run again, increasing her pace as she left the car further behind her. Not until she had gone a couple of hundred yards did she dare come out on the main road.

She had no idea where she was, only that she was somewhere in the countryside, seemingly miles from civilisation. Surely there was a house or a farm nearby where she could seek shelter, or possibly use the telephone and get a car; do anything, in fact, except return to where Larry was waiting for her? He had said he would take her back to London, but she didn't believe him. She had been fool enough to stay for dinner with him, without being more of a fool and going back to him.

In the distance an engine revved and she gave a gasp of fright and ran faster. There was a pain in her side and she pressed her hand to it. The engine was louder now, but it was impossible for her to run any faster. Another moment and it would be on top of her, barring her escape. Headlights blinded her and there was a sharp screech of brakes as she flung herself into the hedge to avoid the impact of a wheel.

'What the hell are you doing in the middle of the road?' a furious voice demanded and, with an exclamation of disbelief, she turned her terror-stricken face and saw Zachary Farrell scowling down at her.

CHAPTER EIGHT

WITHOUT quite knowing how, Samantha found herself sitting beside Zachary in his car, watching silently as he made a skilful turn in the narrow lane and sent the car heading back the way he had come.

'You weren't going in this direction,' she said, surprised.

'But you were.' His tone was abrupt. 'And short of leaving you to my cousin's tender mercies, the only alternative is to drive you to town myself.'

'That's an awful nuisance for you.'

His silence did not add to her comfort and she shifted in her seat. How typical of Zachary not to bother with the convention of social politeness. It *was* a nuisance for him to take her home and he had no intention of pretending otherwise. A half smile curved her mouth. She should know better than to expect him to act out of character. The one thing she had learned so far about Zachary Farrell was that he called a spade a spade. Because of this, many people thought him hard, though far more saw him as forthright and honest.

'I would be more than happy for you to drop me off at the nearest station,' she said into the silence. 'Or even at a garage.'

'You wouldn't be able to hire a car at this time of night.'

'I could try. I feel guilty at making you do a double journey.'

'Forget it,' he said briefly. 'I'll spend the night in town.'

She was annoyed at having forgotten he had a home in London too, and curiosity made her ask him why he hadn't stayed in town anyway, instead of driving back so late.

'I enjoy my weekends in the country,' he explained. 'Besides, I had a feeling my return would be welcomed.'

She digested this, then said slowly: 'Has this sort of thing happened before?'

'Surely you know Larry well enough to have realised that?'

More digestion took place and, reluctant to appear a complete fool, she spoke again with even more honesty. 'I thought you and Marie were staying on with us. Otherwise I wouldn't have agreed to remain here on my own.'

'I wondered about that.' Zachary gave her a quick glance. 'But I wasn't quite sure.'

'You should have given me the benefit of the doubt.'

'Why else do you think I came back? You would have had a long hike to London if I hadn't.'

She shivered and automatically glanced over her shoulder. But there was no car following them, only the empty road stretching behind. 'Do you think Larry's gone back to your home?'

'Probably. I don't expect he'll come chasing after me—if that's what you're asking.'

'Must you sound so smug?'

'I didn't realise I was.' There was surprise in his voice.

'You can't blame me for what happened,' she continued sharply. 'I've been out with Larry quite a few times and he—he's never lunged at me before.'

'You were lucky. You're a beautiful girl, Samantha. I'm sure other men—apart from Larry—have made a pass at you.'

'The others have known when to stop,' she flared.

The car lost speed so suddenly that she jerked forward in her seat.

'You don't mean he——'

'No, I don't,' she cut in. 'But he had a darn good try.'

She was furious to hear a tremble in her voice and it told her she had been more distressed by her scene with Larry than she had realised. Had it happened in London she would have taken it in her stride, but to do battle with a man in a deserted country lane miles from anywhere was not the most pleasant of experiences.

'It was silly of me to get upset,' she murmured. 'But it was unexpected and——'

'Forget it,' Zachary ordered. 'At the very worst you would have ended up with a torn dress. Larry isn't the type to commit rape.'

'Is that a loyal assumption, or do you speak from knowledge?'

A smile quirked his lips. 'I grew up with him. I know him as well as I know myself.'

She wondered if Larry knew Zachary in the same way. Somehow she doubted it. The man beside her had unplumbed depths that few people would be given the chance to fathom.

'If you enjoy your weekends in the country,' she asked, 'why didn't you and Marie stay at the house tonight?'

'Because she's leaving for the States first thing in the morning. Her father has a new play opening on Broadway and she's going over for the first night.'

He lifted his foot off the accelerator as he rummaged in the dashboard pocket and brought out a small silver flask. 'It's brandy,' he explained. 'Have a swig. It will make you feel better.'

'I feel fine, thank you.'

'You're shivering.'

'Only because I'm cold.'

'Why didn't you say so? I can turn on the heater.'

He did so and instantly warm air filled the car. It helped Samantha to relax and she made herself more comfortable. This was the longest time she had spent in Zachary's company and it was amazing how at ease she felt with him. She did not feel impelled to make conversation, nor was she apprehensive when he slowed the car and then stopped. With a deft movement he took off his jacket and slung it over the back seat, then resumed driving.

'Thank you for the compliment,' he said softly.

'What compliment?'

'The one of trust.'

'You aren't the lunging type.'

'That isn't the answer a bachelor likes to hear. You should have said I'm obviously trustworthy and dependable and have iron control!'

'I'm sure you have. But I still can't see you as a wolf.'

'A black sheep, then?'

'A dappled one,' she giggled and, hearing herself laugh, marvelled that she could be having such a light-hearted conversation with Zachary Farrell.

'It was a lovely garden party,' she said, 'and it was awfully kind of you to turn your home upside down for it.'

'I wasn't sure if I was doing the right thing this year,' he admitted. 'I thought the staff might have preferred a dinner in a West End restaurant with dancing and a cabaret.'

'Some of them would,' she said, 'but I think most of them appreciated coming to your home. Maybe you could do both next year.'

'That isn't a very businesslike suggestion.'

'I wasn't thinking of the cost.' She was deflated by his comment. 'Do you always think in monetary terms?'

'If it has to do with business, yes. That's something you must learn as well, Samantha.'

'I'm not a business-woman.'

'You have ten per cent of Farrell's voting stock. I can't think of a better reason for taking an interest in business.'

'I don't intend to keep those shares for ever, Zachary. You know that.'

'Why should I know it?'

Surprise made her give him a direct stare. 'Because I told Larry. I naturally assumed he would tell *you*.'

Zachary's silence told her she had assumed wrongly. Her annoyance with Larry increased. Had he kept the information to himself deliberately or had it been an oversight? Yet why wouldn't he have wanted Zachary to know she intended to return the shares the moment she could?

'You're nearly home,' Zachary said, and she looked up to see they were driving along Sloane Street.

'You've made wonderful time.'

'The weather is good too.'

'I wasn't just making conversation,' she said sharply. 'I meant it.'

'I know. But my answer was meant as a joke.'

The car stopped outside the flat and she swivelled to face him.

'I'm sorry, Zachary, I didn't know. I guess there are a lot of things I don't know about you, but I'm learning all the time.'

'I'm flattered you should want to bother.'

She saw his remark as a warning and in silence opened the door. At once he was beside her on the pavement, walking with her to the entrance of the apartment house.

'I hope that when you come to my home next time,

Samantha, it won't have such an unfortunate end.'

'This end has been very pleasant.' She held out her hand. 'Thank you for being so kind.'

He caught her hand in his large one and held it for a moment. Then with an abrupt 'Goodnight,' he strode across to the car, climbed in and drove off.

Her thoughts were still occupied with Zachary as she let herself into her flat and prepared for bed. What an unexpected end it had been to the evening, and how lucky that Zachary had found her. She remembered why he had said he had not remained in London and felt ridiculously pleased that he had been sufficiently worried about her to think she might need him. Still, it would have been more to the point if he had warned her in the first place. She frowned at her reflection as she finished cleaning her teeth. Had he done so she would have refused to listen. She might even have believed he was trying to make mischief between herself and Larry. Instead of which she now found herself thinking of him in a far friendlier way than she had thought possible when she had gone down to his home this morning.

The telephone rang and she ran across to pick it up, knowing a sharp sense of disappointment as she heard Larry's voice.

'So you're home,' he said without preamble. 'I waited in the car for ages, but when I couldn't see you, I gathered you'd managed to get a lift.'

'With Zachary.'

'The knight errant! How like him to arrive on the scene when he's needed.'

'I gather he's done it before,' she said, her voice as brittle as dry twigs, though it could have been smooth as velvet for all the impression it made on Larry, who gave a low chuckle.

'It's hard to see Zachary as your Sir Galahad, but I

guess that's how you see him tonight.'

'You can hardly blame me,' she said coldly.

'I wasn't going to rape you, Samantha. I only wanted to kiss you.'

Remembering his exploring hands and heavy breathing, she suppressed a shudder.

'I'm sorry about what happened,' he continued. 'My only excuse is that you're a beautiful girl and being near you all day went to my head. I promise it won't happen again.'

'You won't be given the chance.'

'I won't let you put me out of your life,' he said determinedly. 'I know you're still furious with me, but——'

'I'm not furious with you any longer, Larry. But I won't accept any more out-of-town invitations from you.'

'Well, at least you've qualified it.' He sounded pleased. 'Say you forgive me.'

'I forgive you.'

'Can't you sound as if you mean it?'

'I'm tired,' she said abruptly. 'Goodnight.'

'Can I see you tomorrow—it's today now. I'm meeting someone in town for lunch, but I'll be free after four.'

'I won't,' she said quickly, silently vowing not to stay at home in case he took it into his head to call round.

'Then I'll see you on Monday,' he said. 'Goodnight, my beautiful Samantha. Sleep well and think of me.'

'Not if I can help it.' She heard his laugh as she put down the receiver, but as she turned, it rang again and irritably she picked it up. 'Well?' she demanded. 'What do you want now?'

'A friendlier greeting would be a good start.'

Scarlet-faced, she realised it was Zachary. 'I thought it

was your cousin,' she said. 'He just called me to apologise.'

'He does that very well.'

'Do you?'

'I rarely need to apologise.'

'Does being smug come naturally to you, or have you worked on it?' His chuckle was deep and brought such a vivid picture of him to mind that she could imagine him standing in his dressing-gown and pyjamas. 'Where are you?' she asked.

'Round the corner. Are you asking me over?' he said dryly.

'Certainly not!'

'Then in future don't ask me where I am at one o'clock in the morning. It *could* be misconstrued.'

'You would never misconstrue me, Zachary, would you?'

'How flirtatious you've become! It couldn't be because the telephone wire is between us, could it?'

'It could,' she smiled, 'and also because . . .'

'Because?' he questioned.

'Because you rescued me tonight and that's put you in a rather special position in my life.'

'Thank you, Samantha.' He sounded as if he meant it and she racked her brains to find a way of keeping him on the line.

'Did you call me for anything in particular, Zachary?'

'Only to make sure you were all right.'

'I'm fine, thank you.' She paused. 'Are you going back to the country later today?'

'I don't think I fancy the drive again. I have an early appointment up here on Monday morning and I was leaving home at the crack of dawn anyway. It might be as well for me to stay in town.'

'I feel as I've spoiled your weekend,' she said abruptly.

'If you like I—how about coming here for lunch?'

There was a pause, as if it was an invitation he had not expected. But when he spoke, he sounded quite amenable. 'You don't want to be bothered with cooking. Let me take you out instead.'

'It's no bother.'

'I'll pick you up at twelve.' He ignored her comment. 'We can stroll through the park and then have lunch at one of the hotels.'

His goodnight was soft and Samantha was left listening to the purr of the receiver. She gave a little wriggle and felt like purring too. It was oddly exciting to know she would be going out with Zachary.

Samantha changed twice before making up her mind what dress to wear for Sunday morning. She was behaving like a schoolgirl on her first date, and told herself she was only excited because Zachary had always been so unfriendly since they had met. But her logic was at variance with her emotions and her heart was beating loud and fast as noon approached.

The doorbell rang and she forced herself to walk slowly into the hall, her skirts swirling round her shapely legs. She had finally chosen a simple voile dress, not wishing him to think she had taken too much trouble with her appearance. His look was appraising as she opened the door wide. He was as casually dressed as he had been the day before, with an open-necked shirt, denim slacks and a matching blue jacket slung over one shoulder. She stepped back and he followed her into the sitting-room.

'Nice,' he commented.

'I rent it furnished.'

'But the pictures are yours.'

She was surprised at his quick eye. 'How did you know?'

'Furnished flats don't usually run to Burra water-colours.' He paused to peer at one and then walked over to look at a painting of her mother's. 'I have a similar one to this in my flat,' he murmured.

'Which one?'

'Spring in Aldeburgh.'

'That's one of my favourites.'

'You must come over to the flat and see it.'

'That makes a change from etchings,' she said, and saw one of his well-shaped eyebrows lift, before he realised what she meant.

'I promise to keep the front door open all the time,' he said solemnly, 'and my hands in my pockets!'

'You won't need to do that,' she laughed, and then stopped. 'Oh dear, I forgot you wanted me to think of you as a wolf.'

'I've changed my mind.' He eyed her. 'If you're ready, we should go.'

She nodded and, slinging a cardigan over her arm, set off with him for the park.

Families were already picnicking on the grass as they strolled leisurely between the trees in the direction of Park Lane. Children were running around helter-skelter; some with balls or hoops; some with fathers. Samantha glanced shyly at Zachary, wondering what he would say if she suddenly caught hold of his hand. He sensed her eyes were on him and turned to regard her.

'You look very beautiful today, Samantha.'

'Don't I always?'

He laughed. 'Trust a woman never to accept a compliment at face value! Yes, Samantha, you do always look beautiful, but some days you look more beautiful than others. You have lovely hair,' he added. 'It's rare to find such a colour.'

'Not in Sweden or Germany.'

'Even there,' he corrected. 'Swedish blondes tend to be too pale and German ones look like wholesome dairy-maids.'

'Whereas I——?' she teased, and waited to see what simile he would dream up for her.

'Whereas you look like a glass of honey.'

She blushed, amazed that it could be Zachary who was paying her these compliments. A young man and a girl strolled past. She had black hair and reminded Samantha of Marie, who at this moment was somewhere over the Atlantic. Were it not for this, Zachary wouldn't be here now. The knowledge soured Samantha's mood.

'How long will Marie be in America?' she asked.

If he was surprised by her sudden change of subject, he did not show it. 'A couple of weeks. It depends if she's enjoying herself.'

'Won't you mind?'

'I'm not a dog in the manger.'

'Then you can't be the possessive type.'

A smile lightened his face and gave her an idea of what he had been like in his teens.

'Women always think that possessiveness is a sign of love,' he commented. 'Yet in my view it merely shows insecurity.'

'Then *you* would never be jealous,' she said flippantly.

'There have been a few times when I've been insecure,' he said dryly, taking her point. 'But when I was much younger.'

It was easy for her to see him as a lonely boy who had found it difficult to express his feelings. Far different from Larry who, she suspected, had never experienced any such difficulty—if only because his feelings were never deep enough.

'It must be awful to lose your parents when you're young,' she said.

'It's awful at any age.' He quickened his pace, as if he wished to leave his thoughts behind him.

She took the cue and began to run across the grass, her long silver-fair hair bouncing on her shoulders. He caught up with her in a couple of paces and soon outstripped her, pausing some twenty yards ahead to watch as she ran towards him.

'Show-off!' she teased as she rushed forward and, not managing to stop herself in time, bumped into him.

He staggered slightly and his hands came up to grip her. For an instant they remained close and motionless and she felt as if they had been caught in the lens of a camera. Then the shutter clicked and movement started again. She pulled away from him and he stepped to one side and watched as she ran her fingers through her hair to smooth it.

'Leave it,' he commanded. 'I like to see it ruffled.'

'You should see it first thing in the morning.' Colour stained her cheeks and her lids lowered. But he did not tease her because of her remark and instead caught her hand and propelled her forward.

The table he had booked for them was on the top floor of one of the newest hotels and gave them a panoramic view of the city. Haze blurred the most distant outlines and softened the harsh obelisks of skyscrapers. But the people around her were as interesting as the view: afluent middle-aged couples, a spattering of young film types and a fair proportion of tourists, recognisable by their sporty check jackets.

'Do you know this is the first time I've been out to Sunday lunch in a restaurant,' Samantha said. 'It's quite an odd feeling.'

'Are you sure it isn't the company that makes you feel odd?'

'That too.' Head tilted, she surveyed him. 'I like it

when you tease me. Until now I've only seen you as a solemn business-man—the unfriendly Director of Farrell's.'

'Why should that have surprised you?' He leaned his elbows on the table. 'It was a hell of a shock when Uncle John left you those shares. You can't blame me for being suspicious of you when we first met.'

'It went on for longer than that,' she corrected. 'You've been suspicious of me for ages.'

'Because I wasn't sure how you intended to play the game.'

'And now?'

He looked thoughtful. 'Now I think you realise it isn't a game. You know what's at stake. Farrell's isn't just an ordinary department store. It means something to people all over the world. Once anyone has shopped at Farrell's they remember it all their lives.'

'You talk about the store as if it's a woman you love!'

'In a way it is. It's a big proportion of my life.'

'The way it was with Uncle John,' she said, depressed by the thought. 'Surely you want more from your life than that?'

'I'd like a wife and family,' Zachary replied slowly. 'I take it that's what you mean?'

She nodded, trying to see him as a husband and a father. It was easy to do, though she could not see Marie in the role of wife.

'We must order,' he said, and picked up his menu.

It was well after three o'clock when they left the hotel and returned to the park. A slight breeze was blowing and it lifted Samantha's skirts and played a game through the curtain of her hair. It ruffled Zachary's hair too and a dark brown lock fell across his forehead. Several times he pushed it back impatiently, but each time it fell forward again.

'Leave it,' she said finally, repeating what he had said to her a little earlier. 'I like it ruffled.'

'You should have been with me in Hawaii, then. No matter the temperature, there's a continual breeze.'

'My knowledge of Hawaii comes only from television shows,' she said wistfully.

'I had the impression you travelled a lot.'

'To New York and the capitals of Europe. Places where they have important galleries.'

'I don't see you as a hard-bitten agent.'

'I'm not.'

'You mean you weren't.'

'I still *am* my mother's agent,' she corrected. 'I told you I don't intend to keep my ten per cent of Farrell's for a minute longer than necessary.'

'I wasn't sure you meant it. Most women enjoy being in a position of power.'

'What power?' she scoffed. 'You and Larry can outvote me any day.'

'You and Larry have already outvoted *me*!'

She looked away quickly, remembering Marie and the clothes for which Zachary now had to pay the normal wholesale price. The thought of the French girl spoiled her pleasant memories of this afternoon and she quickened her pace. They reached the Sloane Street exit of the park and paused by the kerb for the traffic to ease.

'Even on a Sunday there are traffic jams,' Zachary grumbled. 'It makes me realise how clean the air is in the country.'

'Why don't you commute daily?'

'I will do eventually. For the moment it's more convenient to have a place in town.'

He seemed to sense her change of mood, for he fell silent. It was not the easy, companionable one they had had earlier, but a more wary silence; as if they were sizing each other up and were not quite sure what there was to define. Samantha's apartment building came in sight and she slowed her steps.

'Would you like to come in for a cup of tea?' she asked.

'I can't, I'm afraid. I want to catch up on some paper work.'

'On a Sunday?'

'If there's work to be done, I do it regardless of the day.'

'How single-minded of you!'

'Blame it on my upbringing. I was taught to be conscientious. It was my father's influence.' He saw her questioning look and shrugged. 'He was so grateful that he was allowed to make his home in this country that he always felt he owed it to Britain to give of his best. I'm afraid it's not a popular attitude today.'

'But it's still yours,' she said, and knew it always would be.

He half smiled, drawing her attention to his strong, square jaw. There was nothing effeminate about him; no softness to lessen the determined energy he exuded. Life with him would never be easy, but it would always be exciting. She wished she knew more about him; the friends he had, the life he led and the women he had known before Marie had entered his life. But she dared not ask him. To do so required an intimacy she had not yet attained.

'Thank you for a lovely day, Zachary.' She held out her hand and he took it.

'I should be the one to say thanks. You've made my Sunday in London very pleasant.'

'Since I was responsible for you being here, it was the least I could do.'

'I owe Larry thanks too,' he added.

She was surprised. 'What for?'

'If he'd behaved himself, I would never have had the chance of getting to know you.'

'Do you think you do?'

'Better than I did before. Though I'd never presume to be foolish enough to think one could ever know a woman!'

She laughed. 'You obviously see the female as the Sphinx!'

'And twice as mysterious.' Pressing her hand again, he let it go and walked away.

Her flat seemed lonely when she entered it and the evening stretched interminably ahead of her. She flung open the windows in the sitting-room and went into the kitchenette to make herself a cup of tea. It was at times like this that she wished she was in Ireland with her mother. It was quiet there, but she had never been bored. 'Maybe I'm just a country girl at heart,' she mused, and thought how lovely it would be to live in a house like Zachary's. Quickly she replaced this idea with others that were more innocuous, then picked up the Sunday papers and curled herself up on the settee to read them.

It was not the most exciting prospect for a young woman to be doing on a Sunday evening, but at least there was no problem involved in it, as there might have been had she spent the rest of the day with Zachary.

CHAPTER NINE

SAMANTHA was not surprised when Larry sought her out at mid-morning the next day and reiterated his apology of the day before.

'Forget it,' she said. 'I have.'

'Then why did you refuse to go out with me last night?'

'Because I was going out with someone else.'

'Then come out with me tonight.'

'I'd rather not. It might be as well if we didn't see each other so often,' she added. 'I like you, Larry, but I do have other friends.'

'So have I,' he said easily, 'but I prefer to be with you. I was hoping you felt the same about me.'

'I'm afraid I don't. I hadn't realised I'd given you any other impression.'

'You never refused to go out with me in the past.' He was speaking easily, but there was an undercurrent of irritation in his voice.

'I went out with you because I wanted to get to know you,' she explained. 'After all, we have a business association.' The words reminded her that she was standing in the Millinery Department where she had begun work that morning, and she glanced round to make sure no one was watching them.

'Have lunch with me?' he urged. 'I know it isn't convenient to talk here.'

'We have nothing more to talk about.'

'It's because of Saturday night,' he said. 'You're still angry with me.'

'I'm not—please believe me.'

'I'll only do that when you start going out with me again.' He touched her cheek. 'Don't expect me to take no for an answer.'

'I'd probably be disappointed if you did,' she replied, hoping to soften her refusal, and was relieved to see a customer approaching.

As the day progressed she found her breath catching in her throat each time she caught sight of a dark-haired man. But it always turned out to be a customer or one of the staff, and she left Farrell's that evening without seeing or hearing from Zachary.

This was so for the next three days, and in order to show herself she did not care, she went out with Peter who, to her amusement, spent the best part of the evening talking about Jackie.

'She seems to be thoroughly enjoying herself,' he grumbled, 'and she makes no mention of coming back.'

'I doubt if she will,' Samantha said. 'In her last letter, she wrote and said she's tempted to live there permanently.'

'She'll never do that.' Peter was vehement to hide his disquiet, and Samantha made a mental note to write and tell Jackie that her plan to make Peter miss her might not fail after all.

On Thursday she woke with a dismal feeling which the dark dress she was obliged to wear did nothing to relieve. It was an anachronism for the Farrell staff to wear such dismal clothes and she vowed to discuss it at the next Board meeting. But part of her mood was due to the boredom of working in the Millinery Department, and this was yet another subject she intended to discuss with her co-Directors. With store space at a premium, she was sure the area given over to hats could be far more lucratively employed. It was surprising no one had realised it. Zachary was so aware of everything that went on in the store that ... Darn it, she wasn't going to think of Zachary again. He was most obviously not thinking of *her*!

Slowly the morning dragged by. Two dowagers occupied her for part of the time: trying on countless numbers of hats before eventually buying their usual shapeless pull-ons, which Samantha privately labelled deer-stalkers. A couple of giggling teenagers wandered in—no Farrell customers these, but eager-eyed youngsters looking to see how the other half lived. Once again it made her think what an anachronism this department was. Morosely she wandered over to one of the counters and set an elaborate concoction of satin and straw on a stand. Did anyone wear a hat like this these days, other than the ultra-smart Miss Bergerac? She swung round as her name was called by another of the saleswomen, who pointed to the telephone on the head vendeuse's desk.

Irritated by Larry's persistence, she picked up the receiver and said a sharp hello, almost dropping the instrument as she heard Zachary's voice.

'If you aren't too busy, Samantha, how about joining me for some coffee and sandwiches?'

She glanced at her watch and saw it was nearly her lunch hour.

'I would like that.' Her voice was shaky and she forced herself to draw a deep breath. 'Do you want me to come up right away?'

'Why not? You know where my office is?'

She rushed to the wash-room to make herself tidy, wishing again that she was not wearing drab black, and not noticing how the dark colour enhanced her fairness and the slenderness of her body. She was faintly pink with anticipation when she finally knocked on the door of his room. She had only been here once before—on her first fatal day—and it seemed far longer than two months ago. She sighed. Two months; and Uncle John had wanted her to work here for a year. Somehow she knew she would not be able to stay here for that length of time. Besides, it would not be necessary. She was sure she could work out a compromise with her shares, and then leave Larry and Zachary to run Farrell's by themselves.

But would she be happy to return to her old way of life? Unless she did, her mother would have to find another agent. It might be as well to visit several of the London galleries while she was here and see if she could find someone she liked and trusted to take over from her. Then she would be free to do as she wished: either to return to Ireland and find another job—which meant she could still live at home—or to remain in London.

Zachary rose to greet her and, seeing him coming towards her, his shoulders blocking out the light which shone from the window behind him, she suddenly knew why she did not want to leave England. She was in love with Zachary.

But she hardly knew him. How could he have become so firmly entrenched in her heart that she could not bear the prospect of not seeing him again?

'You're very pensive, Samantha.' Zachary led her to a chair beside his desk. 'I hope you didn't mind me asking you to join me here for lunch? But my next appointment is at two and it doesn't give us time to go to a restaurant.'

'I don't mind at all,' she assured him. 'Though I don't think it's good for you to remain in your office all day.'

'Actually I prefer it. I dislike eating out. At least here I can relax without people watching me.'

'I thought you liked being the centre of attention.'

'I can see that one day I shall have to give you a résumé of my character.'

'I look forward to that,' she smiled.

'How about this evening, then? Again it's short notice, I'm afraid, but if you're free...'

She knew she should say she was busy, but because she wanted to go out with him, she nodded.

'That's settled, then. I'll pick you up when I leave here.'

'I would like to go home and change first.'

'You look fine to me.' He saw from her face that he had said the wrong thing, and looked so wry that she laughed.

'You can't honestly say I look as nice as I did on Saturday or even Sunday.'

'You look different,' he agreed. 'But you are one of the few girls I know who look good in black. Most women look dreary in it.'

He sat down beside his desk and signalled her to pour out the coffee. A plate of assorted sandwiches stood beside the silver pot and there were two small jugs of milk and cream.

'You're deceptively efficient,' he went on, following his own train of thought. 'I've been surprised by the way you've settled down and the suggestions you've made to the various departments.'

'You know about them?'

'Madame Vonet has been to see me twice,' he said dryly. 'She's quite a fan of yours.'

'Only after she found out who I was!'

His teeth flashed in a smile. 'You must at least give her credit for turning her coat so quickly!'

Samantha bit into a sandwich. It was as tasty as it looked, but only a bite-sized helping. 'This isn't much of a lunch for you,' she commented.

'Meaning big strong men should eat big strong meals?'

'Exactly.'

'I prefer to lunch sparingly. Then I can enjoy a leisurely dinner. Which reminds me—do you have any preference in restaurants?'

'Not really. Where do you usually go?'

He paused, then said slowly: 'I'd like to take you somewhere new. How early can you be ready?'

'By half past six. You must let me change first,' she insisted.

'I'll give you a lift home.'

'Fine,' she said easily, and offered him another sandwich.

Two cups of coffee later, she stood up to leave, thinking he would appreciate a chance to relax on his own before his afternoon appointments began. She noticed how tired he looked and knew it must be a great responsibility to run a store like this. Still, he had Larry to help him.

'Why don't you and Larry split the work more evenly?' she asked bluntly.

'We're too diametrically opposed,' he replied. 'I'd spend half my time trying to undo the decisions he had made, and he'd be doing the same with mine! Anyway, he's far better than I am at taking care of the personnel. I don't get on with people.'

'I don't believe that. I'm sure you could get on with anyone if you wanted to.'

'Perhaps I don't want to,' he said humorously. 'Anyway, think of the work I do that Larry couldn't do—even if he were willing to try. And don't say it's because I won't let him!'

'Why should I say that?'

'Because many people do.'

'Then they don't know Larry,' she stated. 'He isn't as interested in Farrell's as you are.'

'You're perceptive.' Zachary's voice was toneless. 'Or

has he said anything to you about it?'

She hesitated. 'I know he's more keen on racing. He's working on some invention that will save petrol.'

'He's been working on that for a couple of years,' Zachary said. 'That's why he resents any time he has to spend at the store. It's one of the areas of contention between us. He'll never succeed if he's half-hearted. If he really believes in that invention of his, he should go all out on it.'

'He'd need a lot of money,' she replied. 'It would mean selling some of his shares in Farrell's.'

'I know.'

'Surely you would hate him to do that?'

'Not if he sold them to me.'

Her eyes widened. 'But that would mean giving you control.'

'So what?' Zachary looked and spoke impatiently. 'If he doesn't give a damn about Farrell's—and I assure you he doesn't, apart from the money it brings in for him—then why shouldn't he sell out to me?'

'No reason at all,' she said, with a growing awareness of the rightness of what he was saying. 'And it would be marvellous for me too. Then I wouldn't be the lynch-pin any longer. I'd be free.'

'No one is ever free.' He came towards her. 'Even a bird has to return to his flock.'

'A cuckoo doesn't!'

'You're no cuckoo. And you would never have to steal a nest, either. You will always find one of your own.'

Smiling, she skirted her chair to go to the door. He moved at the same time and his arm brushed against hers. A tingle went through her and she glanced at him. They were close enough for her to see how distinctively curved his eyebrows were and how thick the lashes that bordered his light grey eyes.

With no hint of what he was going to do, he leaned down and kissed her on the mouth. Instinctively she responded, and he put his hands on her shoulders and pulled her closer still. He kissed her a second time, his lips warmer, the pressure more insistent. She wanted him to go on kissing her and, because she was dismayed by the thought, she pulled away from him.

'You choose the oddest times to kiss a girl,' she said lightly.

'The time rather chose me.' His voice was very deep. 'You're rather like water, Samantha. Before one can guard against you, you've penetrated everywhere.'

She would have liked to ask him what he meant, but knew from the way he walked to the door that he would not answer her. Remembering she would be meeting him later, she was content to bide her time.

In the event Zachary did not take her home, sending her a message via his secretary that he was unavoidably detained in a meeting and would collect her at six-thirty. In a way she was glad. She was tired and grimy and did not wish him to see her until she had bathed and changed. It was strange to feel such a sense of excitement and to know it was caused by Zachary, the last man in the world with whom she had seen herself falling in love.

No longer did she try to deny it. How could she when her whole body trembled at the mere thought of him. But why now, after two months? Why not the first time they had met? She remembered the antagonism he had aroused in her on that first occasion and, with hindsight, saw it had been an instinctive reaction, caused by fear. Even then she must have sensed the power he would eventually have over her. She saw now that in going out with Larry she had hoped to bring herself to Zachary's attention. Well, she had his attention, but where it was going to lead her was a question she could not answer. Probably nowhere, she thought miserably. He was only taking her out because Marie was in New York.

It was an unpleasant admission, but she refused to let it sour her mood and was sweetness itself as she opened the door to his ring. Her skin was flushed from her bath, her hair still faintly damp, with the ends curling softly under. She wore more make-up than usual—almost as if it were a mask behind which she could hide—and she felt Zachary give her a startled look as he stepped into the hall. He too looked different tonight: very broad in a light grey suit, his neck rising tanned and strong from a pale blue shirt whose colour lent blue depths to his clear grey eyes. She was curious to know where he was taking her, but did not ask, even pretending not to notice when he started to drive out of London.

Their destination turned out to be a riverside restaurant whose dining-room overlooked lawns that sloped down to the water.

'The setting is simple, but the food is excellent,' Zachary assured her, and she wondered what he would say if she told him that even eating straw with him would be palatable.

'Straw is just right for me,' she reflected. 'It shows what a donkey I am!' Deliberately she studied him over her pre-dinner drink, trying to assess what there was about him that made him so special to her. There were many things that set him apart from the other men she knew: his looks, his seriousness, his acute mind. It was hard to understand why Uncle John had not left him control of Farrell's.

'Henri Bergerac's play had excellent reviews in New York,' she said, forcing herself to bring the name Bergerac into the conversation.

'He got a standing ovation in the theatre,' Zachary added. 'Marie told me.'

'Is she back?' The question was almost whispered.

'No. I spoke to her on the telephone.'

Samantha longed to ask how often he did so, but bit hard on her lip instead.

'Shall we order?' he suggested.

'Why the hurry?'

'I've got plans,' he teased and, at her questioning look, nodded his dark head in the direction of the river. 'I've always fancied myself in a punt with a pretty girl.'

'I'm not a good swimmer,' she warned.

'Thanks for your vote of confidence!'

Laughing, they opened the menu. By the time they entered the dining-room it was already full, though they seemed to be the only people from out of town. The food was as delicious as Zachary had promised and she asked him how he had come to hear of the place.

'An American brought me here the first week it opened and I've been meaning to come back ever since.'

He poured the wine which had been set before them and they lapsed into easy conversation. It was still light when they drank their final cup of coffee and then made their way to the water's edge and the punt which was awaiting them.

'I thought you were joking,' she murmured as she gingerly stepped into it.

'I never joke about serious things.' He gave his attention to negotiating his way and it was several moments before he relaxed.

They were moving slowly upstream. On either side of them gardens meandered down to the water's edge, with houses set further back: gracious houses that looked as if they had come off the covers of *Homes & Gardens*.

'I'd love a place on the river,' she said.

'It can be rather damp in the winter,' he said prosaically.

'How unromantic you are!'

His eyes glinted, making comment unnecessary, and she looked away hurriedly and trailed her hand in the water. As it grew dusk they returned to the small lounge where fresh coffee and home-made biscuits were served to them. Another young couple sat opposite, hands linked, eyes locked, then moving slowly—as if in a dream—they rose and went up the narrow, timbered staircase.

Zachary met Samantha's eyes and gave a faint smile. 'They have a few bedrooms here. It's a way of earning extra money.'

'I wouldn't have thought it paid.'

'People are always looking for somewhere secluded to stay.'

She felt her cheeks burn and hoped the light was too poor for him to see. But it was a vain hope, as his next words told her.

'I only brought you here to dinner, Samantha. My car isn't likely to break down and even if it did, we could hire a taxi.'

She set her cup sharply on the tray. 'I'm not scared, Zachary. I know the way I behaved on Saturday didn't show it, but as I said at the time, it was only because it was so unexpected.'

'You still looked somewhat big-eyed when the couple opposite went upstairs.'

'That was unexpected too.'

'Why? When a couple love each other, what's more natural than for them to want to go to bed?'

For a split second she was startled, then she laughed. 'You're quite right.'

'Then why the embarrassment?' he persisted.

'Because I'm with *you,*' she said flatly. 'You've always been so serious with me that I—that I can't——'

'Think of me as a lover?' he cut in.

Because the exact opposite was true she became even more flustered. But luckily he too saw it to mean the opposite.

'I may be the serious type, Samantha, but I'm not a monk—as you well know.'

No words could more quickly have brought her down to earth, and she gathered her bag on to her lap, a sign he read correctly by rising and suggesting they leave.

Throughout the journey back to London his foot did not leave the accelerator, and he only stopped when they reached her apartment building. Afraid he believed she had wanted to end the evening because she had not enjoyed it, she searched for a way of showing him this was not true.

'Would you like to come in for a nightcap? It isn't all that late.'

'Sounds a good idea,' he agreed, and followed her to the lift. Outside her door he took the key from her, inserted it in the lock and went in ahead of her to switch on the lights in the hall. Together they entered the living-room. It was almost as if they were returning to their own home, with Zachary playing the part of her husband. Samantha dropped her bag and jacket on to a chair and ran her hands through her hair. It was silky to the touch and she pulled it slowly to try and make herself less aware of the nervousness coursing through her.

'Coffee or whisky?' she asked in a high voice.

'Neither,' he said thickly, and put his arms round her.

With a sigh she gave herself up to his hold, knowing this was what she had been waiting for since he had come to collect her five hours ago.

There was nothing fumbling or inexpert in his touch.

It was that of an experienced man who knew how to arouse without creating fear. It was amazing how intimate the touch of mouth upon mouth could be; the way lips could move with sensual deliberation, arousing a hundred unknown senses; turning her strength to weakness and her will-power to water. Her legs trembled and he gathered her closer, drawing her down upon the settee and cradling her on his lap. The musky scent of his after-shave lotion was heady in her nostrils and mingled with the warm smell of his skin. His hair was soft to her touch and she rubbed her hand against it. He responded by doing the same to hers, then his fingers moved down her cheek to clasp her throat. They didn't go any further but remained on the base of her neck, his thumb moving softly upon the pulse that beat there.

She longed to say something to him but was afraid she would give herself away. Instead she contented herself by murmuring his name over and over again as if it were a mantra. Zachary was silent too, save for the odd incoherent little whisper. She wondered if he too were afraid of giving away his thoughts or if he were keeping quiet because there was nothing he wanted to say; because for him this was merely the culmination of a pleasant evening; a kiss of propinquity and not love. It was a depressing thought and she pulled back from him. She was crazy to become involved with a man who already had a mistress. Another girl-friend would have been hard enough to compete with, but a woman whom he actually kept was impossible to fight.

She saw him looking at her, his eyes a darker grey in the soft light that came from the shaded lamps.

'Let's try it again,' he said huskily, but when he went to draw her close, she stiffened. Instantly he became motionless. 'You said you weren't scared of me.'

'I'm not.'

'Then relax.' He remained with his shoulders leaning against the settee behind him. 'I find myself in an unexpected position with you,' he continued softly, 'though on Saturday night I had a feeling it would end like this.'

'Why should our friendship end just because you've kissed me?' she asked with pretended naïvety.

'Is that how you read my remark? I didn't mean it that way. What I'm actually trying to say is that when I first met you I didn't realise I would become fond of you. And for God's sake don't take exception to that remark!'

'Why should I?' she said. 'The word "fond" makes me feel safe and secure.'

'Now you're getting at me,' he replied, and gave her a teasing look which went well with his sensual mouth. 'I would like to see more of you,' he went on. 'Much more.'

'Physically or in terms of hours?' she asked blandly.

'Both, you saucy minx!' His voice deepened. 'But it won't affect our business relationship if you refuse.'

'I didn't know we had a business relationship.'

'You're in an important position at Farrell's. I don't think you realise it.'

'I'd prefer not to. It would make me uncomfortable.' She sat up and swung her legs to the ground, a movement as graceful as her pale blonde appearance.

'When you were lying down you looked like a child,' he said, with a note of surprise in his voice and, reaching out, touched a strand of her hair. 'It's surprisingly thick. Most blondes have fine hair.'

'Are you speaking from experience?'

'Of course. The average blonde has some twenty thousand fewer hairs than a brunette, while redheads have even less.'

'About ninety thousand,' she said demurely.

'You read that article in *The Times* too!' He rose and she laughed and made a face at him, which prompted him to hug her, a gesture that was friendly and without passion. 'I had a wonderful evening with you, Samantha. Will you let me repeat it?'

'Which part?'

'Both,' he said, echoing his previous answer. 'Though if I have a choice I'll take the latter half.'

'Not quite half,' she corrected, glancing at her watch.

'You're the one who's turning me out,' he said promptly and, pausing by the door, kissed the tip of her nose.

Did he always like to make love to a girl at the end of a pleasant evening? she wondered, as she bolted the door behind him. If he did it would be safer for her not to go out with him again. Zachary was seeing her because Marie was in America and only when the girl returned would she herself know exactly where she stood in his life. Sighing audibly, she prepared for bed.

CHAPTER TEN

FOR the whole of the next day Samantha was keyed up in the expectation of hearing from Zachary. But the entire day passed without word from him and by five-thirty she went to the cloakroom to change into the light cotton dress which she had brought with her, having found it too depressing to leave here every day in her drab black uniform. She really must talk to Larry about it.

She was still preoccupied with this when she walked out of the staff entrance and did not notice a small black car keeping pace with her until it hooted. Looking round, she saw Zachary behind the wheel. Instantly the sky was bluer, the setting sun warmer as she hurried to the kerb to greet him.

'Get in,' he said with a smile. She did so, looking so guilty that he chuckled. 'I'm sure that by now everyone knows who you really are.'

'Do you think so?'

'Farrell's have a grapevine louder than a tom-tom. Apart from which, you sat at the Directors' table at the staff party.'

'I'd forgotten that.'

'I bet you forgot me too?'

'No, I didn't.' She was so happy she could have flung her arms wide. 'I didn't think I was going to see you today,' she confessed.

'I know you don't like me to call you during working hours,' he mocked.

'You could always pretend it was business,' she said solemnly.

'Monkey business,' he replied, and reached out to squeeze her fingers. His hand remained on her lap for a moment and she felt its weight against the top of her leg. She trembled and he moved his hand quickly back to the wheel.

'It's rude of me to assume you are free tonight,' he said quietly, 'but if you are, will you take pity on me?'

'A bachelor in need of pity?' she teased, hoping he would say something about Marie. But he didn't, and she was forced to continue: 'Shall I play hard to get and say I'm busy, or should I admit that the whole week stretches ahead of me without a single date?'

'I wouldn't believe you if you said *that*.'

'It's true, though. But through inclination.'

'You don't need to tell me that,' he assured her. 'I'm quite willing to believe you can go out every night of the week if you choose.' He negotiated his way past a bus. 'If you don't need to go back to your flat I can take you straight to mine. Unless you'd prefer to go out somewhere?'

She was not sure she wanted to go to his flat. The one thing she didn't want Zachary to think was that he could make love to her when the mood took him and then drop her like a hot potato once Marie came back into his life. Yet to say this would be leaving herself open to a rebuff, and she was wondering how to phrase it when he spoke again.

'Perhaps it might be best if I took you out. It's more fun for you to go to a restaurant.'

'I'm quite happy to be with you.'

'That's settled, then,' he said so quickly that she knew this was what he had wanted.

He did indeed live around the corner from her, as he had said, but in an extremely elegant block. The main windows of his living-room afforded a beautiful view of the park, and though it was not on the top floor, it had a large terrace set with garden furniture and a hammock. Window boxes ran along its entire length and Samantha marvelled at the beautiful display of flowers.

'By courtesy of Farrell's,' he said. 'Our Gardening Department designed the terrace for me and takes care of it.'

'I knew they planned gardens, but I didn't realise they took care of them.'

'Only mine,' he said, and gave her a quizzical look. 'I hope you won't bring that up at our next Board meeting!'

Red-faced, she looked at him. 'I would do the same

again about Marie's clothes. It was the principle to which I objected.'

'Not the fact that I was the one doing it?'

'No,' she said firmly, and then added with honesty: 'I might not be so unbiased now.'

His look became more quizzical. 'I didn't know you were the jealous type.'

'All women are jealous,' she said defensively. 'It doesn't mean anything. It's just an instinct.'

'Like animals and their determination to keep their territory from being invaded?' he suggested.

'That's it exactly.' Quickly she changed the subject. 'I'd like to have a wash if I may.'

'Of course.' He led her back through the lounge, which was spacious and furnished in muted shades of green and beige, and into a guest suite. 'I think you'll find everything you want here,' he said. 'If not, give me a call.'

Without moving, she watched as he went out and closed the door, then looked carefully around her. The room was charmingly furnished and had an air of use about it; a fact which she noted wryly, since it suggested Marie or any other young woman who took his fancy.

In the bathroom she found everything she could possibly want in the way of make-up. There were also three different kinds of scent, a freshly laundered bath-robe and even electrically heated hair-curlers. She examined the make-up carefully, pulling a face as she saw several shades of lipstick, powder and eye-shadow. Zachary obviously believed in catering for different women and, if the make-up was anything to go by, he was somewhat eclectic in his taste.

She would have liked to have had a shower, but decided this would take too long, satisfied herself with a wash and a re-application of lipstick and mascara. Her pale skin was tanned light honey and needed no powder, though she added a touch of shadow to her lids to highlight her grey eyes. How large and shiny they looked: the glitter of excitement and fear. Quickly she went back into the hall.

Zachary was coming out of his own room and she had a glimpse of a dark blue carpet and blue-covered bed. Seeing her look, he opened his door wider.

'You're quite safe with me before dinner,' he said, beckoning her forward.

With a toss of her head she stepped past him into his room. This too looked out over the park and was much larger than the guest room. The bed was king-sized and she averted her eyes from it as she went to the window. The decor was simple yet luxurious: the richness of navy velvet lightened with acid yellow and white.

'Your taste,' she asked, 'or Farrell's?'

'Farrell's. I merely told them what sort of bed I wanted.'

'That doesn't surprise me,' she said, showing him he was not going to embarrass her so easily. He guessed that was her intention, for his eyebrows rose wickedly as he asked her if she would like to test the mattress. 'I had it especially sprung for me,' he explained.

'Do you have a bad back, then?' she asked, wide-eyed.

'I would have had, if I hadn't ordered the bed!' Deciding he had teased her enough, he led her back into the lounge. 'Let me know when you're ready to eat.'

'Right now I can do with a drink.'

He mixed her a Tom Collins and set a plate of canapés in front of her.

'Yummy!' she said, tasting one. 'Made by your own fair housekeeper's hands, of course?'

'Of course.'

'Does she live in?'

He shook his head. 'She comes each day. She'd live in

if I asked her, but I don't need it at the moment.'

'Do you do much entertaining here?'

'I prefer restaurants. I keep my home for my personal friends.'

She was warmed by his compliment and made no protest when he pulled her across the settee to rest against him. She knew he wanted to kiss her and realised he was waiting for her to show she wanted him to do so. Deliberately she remained quiescent against him, determined not to give him the sign he wanted, and only realising she had become rigid when he gave her a gentle shake and told her to relax.

'I am relaxing,' she protested, and half turned her face up to his.

'Maybe this will help you to relax more,' he whispered, and tilted her face higher so that her lips were just below his own. 'Darling Samantha,' he breathed, and with unexpected passion began to kiss her.

Quickly she responded, wondering where her coolness had gone, yet not regretting its disappearance. Whatever happened in the future she would have this moment to remember. Perhaps if she could infiltrate into his life she would be able to carve a niche in it for herself before Marie returned? She waited for the thought of the girl to dismay her, but, held close against Zachary, it was easy to forget anyone else. It was herself he was holding, her body he was touching, her skin he was caressing with his lips. Many different emotions welled inside her, but the strongest was the primaeval urge to be possessed. For the first time with him she became afraid—not of Zachary but of her own weakness. Quickly she put her hands to his chest and pushed.

He moved back from her. Not too far; only sufficiently for him to look into her face.

'Such big eyes, Samantha.' His voice was so deep it

seemed to come from somewhere low in his chest.

'I'm not frightened of *you*,' she confessed, 'but of myself.'

His look was tender, as were the kisses he placed on her eyelids before he rose and went across to the sideboard to pour himself a drink.

'Lots of ice,' he murmured, 'though the way I feel now I could melt the North Pole! You are an extremely desirable female.'

'Maybe you rouse easily!'

'I've never thought so.' He came across to her but took a chair, as if he didn't trust himself to sit on the settee beside her. 'I generally have to work myself up into the mood. Drinks to relax me, candlelight to soothe me, a bed on which I can fall comfortably ... But with you ... Just looking at you in the car in the middle of a stream of traffic makes my mind start to play tricks on my body.'

His voice was matter-of-fact though his words were anything but, and as she dropped her eyes from his face to his hands, she saw a slight tremor in them. So he was not talking for effect. He really did mean what he said.

'I don't think Marie would be overjoyed to hear this conversation.' She had not meant to say this, yet she was glad she had, even though he looked startled.

'Nor would my other girl-friends.'

'I didn't know you had more than one at a time!'

'That's what a gentleman always likes a lady to believe!'

'You're playing with words, Zachary.'

'Maybe it isn't the time to be serious.'

There was no doubt this was a rebuff and she reacted to it by jumping to her feet and walking over to the dining alcove. 'I'm hungry. Let's eat.'

If he saw through the excuse, he gave no sign and held

out a chair for her to sit down. The meal was excellent. There was ice-cold gazpacho, salmon trout and salad, lemon mousse and assorted cheeses.

'I know Farrell's didn't prepare the food,' she said when, supper over, they sipped their coffee on the terrace, 'but they certainly provided it.'

'What makes you say that?'

'The quality.'

'I'm proud of our Food Hall,' he admitted. 'As you know, I would like to expand it.'

'Get rid of Millinery.'

'I need more space on the ground floor. The second floor is no good to me. That's why I want to build the annex.'

'What else will you put in it?'

'I haven't decided. I have an open mind.'

'That must be unusual!'

'Now, now,' he reproved. 'You're supposed to be my friend.'

'That doesn't mean I'm blind to your faults.'

'Do you honestly think I have a closed mind?'

'I think you can be obstinate,' she said thoughtfully, 'and I'm not sure if you like to admit when you're wrong.' She put down her cup. 'Now you can be unflattering about me.'

His lower lip jutted forward as he surveyed her. 'Do you know,' he said slowly, 'I don't think there's anything about you I don't like.'

'I can't believe that,' she protested.

'It's true. I'm sure you have faults, but at the moment they are all lovable ones. Even the fact that you made me pay a higher price for Marie's clothes, I see only as your desire to play fair to the other Directors.'

She was surprised he should refer to this incident so lightly and was piqued that he had no embarrassment in mentioning Marie. 'Maybe it will teach you not to be so generous next time,' she said flippantly. 'Or do you always keep your girl-friends in dresses?'

'I would prefer to keep them without,' he grinned. 'And to answer your question, Miss Nosey Parker, I didn't set out to pay for Marie's wardrobe. She just happened to see a dress she liked in Farrell's and I told her to get it. After that, it accelerated.'

'Like Topsy,' Samantha smiled. 'It just growed!'

'I'll call a halt one day,' he shrugged.

She thought he must be extremely rich not to have called a halt before now, but knew it was not her business to comment on his finances.

'Why are we talking about Marie?' he said huskily. 'All I want to talk about is you.' He reached out for her and with a sharp movement pulled her across the space that divided them and on to his lap. 'And not much talking either,' he continued. 'I can think of better things to do.'

Once again he started to kiss her. There was no strangeness in his touch and she knew with a despairing admission that she had found her final heaven. If only she could believe that Zachary had found it too!

It was midnight before he drove her home, explaining that he had a business dinner the following evening and would see her the night after.

'That's Friday,' she said. 'Aren't you going down to the country for the weekend?'

'Only if you'll come with me.'

She resisted the temptation and shook her head.

'I thought you wouldn't,' he said regretfully. 'Is it because you don't trust me?'

'I don't trust *us*,' she corrected.

'If I can rustle up some friends, will you come then?'

'I would love to.'

'Take it as done.' He brought her hand up to his lips and kissed it and then let it go.

On Friday morning Larry came in search of her. Samantha had not seen him since the previous Saturday and, looking into his handsome face, wondered why she was in love with Zachary and not his younger cousin. Larry was easier to understand and also easier to cope with.

'Hello,' she said lightly. 'Long time no see.'

'That's your fault, not mine. I've rung you several evenings this week, but you haven't been in.'

'I've been busy.'

He looked sour. 'With Zachary, I gather.'

'Yes.'

'And this weekend too?'

'Are you checking up on me?' she asked.

'Zachary told me himself. I wanted to go down for the weekend, but he said the house would be full.'

'Poor Larry,' she teased. 'Are you feeling left out in the cold?'

'That isn't funny, Samantha. You know I'm keen on you—I've made that very plain.'

'I'm sure you'll be equally keen on another girl next month.' She put her hand on his arm. 'I'm sorry, Larry, but it's much better if we don't see so much of each other.'

'It isn't better for me.' He put his hand over hers as it rested on his arm. She tried to pull it away, stopping in surprise as she saw Zachary coming towards them. She tugged at her hand again, but Larry still held on to it, only releasing it as his cousin came abreast of them.

'Not interrupting you both, am I?' Zachary said quietly.

'Larry was just going,' she said pointedly, and gave the younger man such a sharp look that he grinned.

'I'll see you later,' he said. 'Don't forget me.'

'Do you want me for anything?' Samantha asked Zachary the moment they were alone.

'No. At least, I ...' He frowned. 'What were you and Larry whispering about?'

'No secrets,' she said. 'We were only whispering because we didn't want anyone else to hear.' She gave Zachary a sidelong glance, pleased to see him scowling. Perhaps a bit of jealousy might be good for him. It could have a cathartic influence on his mind and help to clear it of other women.

'Larry is annoyed because I'm seeing so much of you,' she admitted. 'And he's particularly cross about this weekend.'

'You can always cry off if you wish.'

She faced him squarely. 'Are you saying that because you're angry or because you're jealous?'

He scowled even harder, but she went on staring at him, and after a few seconds the scowl left his face and he smiled slightly.

'I'm sorry, Samantha. I asked for that. But I was in a foul mood.'

'Why?'

'Because I'm jealous and I don't like it.'

'You have no need to be jealous of Larry. I haven't been out with him since the garden party.'

'You'd still be going out with him if he hadn't frightened you.'

'And you'd still be going out with Marie if she weren't in New York! Honestly, Zachary, be adult about it.' Though angered by his inability to see she had stopped going out with Larry because she loved Zachary himself, she tried to retain her control. 'I went out with Larry because he kept asking me and was always friendly to me. I'd have gone out with you for the same reason—if you'd asked me first.'

'I asked you the first week you were here, but you refused.'

'Because I already had a date,' she retorted. 'And you didn't ask me again until last week.'

'Are you going out with me to show me how unbiased you are?'

Astonishment took away her anger. 'If you think that, we'd better stop seeing each other.' She turned her back on him. 'You can tell Larry you'll have room for him at your home this weekend. He can take my place.'

'No one can take your place,' Zachary said, his breath tickling her ear. 'I must be going mad, Samantha. You make me say things I don't mean.' His hand was light upon her shoulder. 'Please turn round and look at me.'

Slowly she obeyed. Their eyes met and he muttered something and drew back as a customer came in their direction.

'If I stay here any longer I'll kiss you,' he whispered shakily. 'I'll see you later.'

He strode away, pausing some yards distant to talk to another saleswoman. Samantha watched him, enjoying the sight of his dark, distinctive face. How he dominated everyone around him by the strength of his personality! It was also clear that he was the brains behind all the new ideas that had been put into operation since Uncle John's death. The more she learned about Zachary, the more incomprehensible it was that he had not been given control of Farrell's. Was it because Larry was the son of Uncle John's twin that her godfather had found it impossible not to give him an equal part of the business? This seemed the only logical reason and she wished he had not seen fit to put her in the centre of what she felt could become an unpleasant family situation.

However, her weekend in Zachary's country house was exceeded by her highest expectations. She drove down with him late on Friday afternoon, arriving shortly before the two other couples he had invited. One of them brought their two children and she was delighted by the way Zachary played with the youngsters, showing a lightheartedness that gave another dimension to his personality.

The weather was excellent for most of the time, though on Saturday evening there was a thunderstorm and they sat in the rustic sitting-room, playing Scrabble and various other games that Zachary brought out.

On Sunday the weather was glorious again and they lounged by the pool. Zachary disappeared shortly afterwards, a fact which spoiled Samantha's pleasure in the pool and the company, though she tried not to show it.

'Don't tell me you had work you couldn't put off?' she said coldly as he finally joined them at noon and dived into the water to swim beside her.

'I wasn't working in the real sense of the word. I was in my workroom.'

'With your tables and chairs.'

'With my tables and chairs,' he smiled.

'You're very unsociable.'

Annoyed that he had not wished to be with her, she lunged forward, though she managed to have a smile on her face as she reached the side of the pool. Not waiting for Zachary to join her, she heaved herself up and sat on the edge. He swam leisurely across to her and with a lithe bound was beside her, the water gleaming on his body and clinging to the thick hair that lay across his chest.

He eyed her, then leaned forward and placed his lips

on her shoulder. They were warm on her skin and sent a delicious shiver through her body. Her anger disappeared. It was mean of her to be upset because Zachary had wanted to spend time in his workroom. It was his way of relaxing and no doubt it did him more good than having to make conversation with other people.

'If you want to go back to your woodwork this afternoon,' she said quickly, 'I'm sure your friends won't mind.'

'What about you?'

'I won't mind either. Honestly.'

'You're sweet,' he said huskily. 'But I've finished for the day.'

After tea the two couples and the children departed. Samantha waited to see what time Zachary suggested they left and wondered if he would ask her to spend the night here and return to London in the morning. What would she say if he did? Nervously she considered one answer after another then, not finding the right one, discarded them all.

'I thought we'd leave about nine,' he said into the silence. 'We'll be home by eleven and you won't have too late a night.'

'You mean after my hectic weekend?' She was so delighted that he hadn't asked her to stay that she gave him a dazzling smile. 'I've never had such a lazy two days.'

'But enjoyable, I hope?'

'You know I've loved every minute of it.'

'The house and garden *are* rather nice,' he said.

'So is the owner of them.'

'Only nice?'

'Irresistible,' she smiled.

'Is that why you keep saying no to me?'

'You haven't asked me.'

'And if I did?'

'I'd say no!'

His laugh was spontaneous and he looked young and without a care in the world.

The sky was darkening as they headed back to town, driving in a bigger car this time and leaving the small one behind. 'I'm taking a few things back with me,' Zachary explained at her questioning look, but did not vouchsafe more until he arrived at her flat, when he opened the boot and took out the little rosewood table she had seen the week before. Even in the light of a street lamp it was beautiful, the marquetry top forming a precise and intricate pattern.

'For you,' he said, and held it out to her.

She took it, but he still kept hold of the weight.

'You—you c-can't mean that,' she stammered. 'It must have taken you hours of work.'

'I finished it this morning,' he said, and all at once she knew why he had spent all those hours in his workroom away from her.

'And I was angry with you because of it,' she said huskily. 'You knew, didn't you?'

'Yes, but I wasn't hurt. Only flattered that you missed me.' He went up with her in the lift. 'Where would you like to put the table?' he asked. 'In the living-room?'

'No—I'll have it in my bedroom. Then I can put my books on it.'

She opened the door of her room before realising it was the first time he had seen where she slept. Blushing, she hurriedly pushed her chiffon nightdress under the pillow, though he could still see it as he set the table by the bed.

'It will be right beside you when you sleep,' he said huskily.

'And beside me when I wake up.'

'Where I would like to be.'

'Zachary.' She took a half-step towards him and he did the same. Then they stopped. His mouth twitched and then clamped tight.

'No,' he said in a strangled voice, 'there's a limit even to *my* self-control.' Turning his back on her, he strode to the front door. 'I won't be able to see you tomorrow night. Marie is coming back and I promised to meet her.'

His words were like a douche of cold water and it was several seconds before she could speak. 'You don't need to make excuses not to see me, Zachary.'

'It isn't an excuse; just an explanation.'

'You don't need to give me any explanation either.'

'Don't you want to know why I can't see you?' he asked roughly.

'Not if the answer concerns Marie,' she said evenly. 'Your diplomacy is slipping.'

'I don't want to be diplomatic with you. I want to be honest.'

It was difficult to cap this, so she pretended to stifle a yawn.

He took the hint and stepped into the outside hall. 'I'll call you, Samantha.'

She nodded and closed the door, then swiftly opened it again.

'The table is wonderful. I'll—I'll always cherish it, Zachary.'

Her voice cracked and she closed the door and rested her head against it. Why did Marie have to come back so soon? If she had stayed away another week Zachary might have fallen in love with her. Yet the thought brought no comfort. She didn't want Zachary to love her just because Marie was away. She wanted a genuine love; one that would last and deepen. No, it was better for the girl to return. At least then she and Marie would know where they stood. Blinking back her tears, she bolted the door. But perhaps neither of them mattered seriously to him. It was a dismal thought and her tears flowed faster, making it impossible for her to stop them.

CHAPTER ELEVEN

WHETHER it was fate or because he knew Zachary would be otherwise engaged, Larry sought out Samantha on Monday morning and asked her to have dinner with him. Reluctant to be alone and think of Zachary smiling into Marie's pert little face, she accepted the offer.

By the time Larry came to pick her up, she regretted having agreed to go out with him. It was an effort to pretend to a cheerfulness she did not feel and she drank two champagne cocktails quickly, pleased when they gave a lift to her spirits. Larry set out to amuse her and did not refer to his cousin until they were halfway through dinner; and only then because he had had a row with him earlier in the day and was still upset by it.

'I was hoping he'd buy a big block of my shares, he informed her, 'but he won't.'

'Why not?' She was astonished. 'He wants to have control of the store, doesn't he?'

'He says he can't pay the price I want.'

'Can't he raise the money?'

'He won't. He says my price is too high.'

'Is it?'

Larry hesitated, then shrugged. 'I have someone who is willing to pay me treble the face value if I sell out my *entire* holding.'

She thought what this would mean to Zachary and said carefully: 'Uncle John would have hated to think of you selling out.'

'I know. But you can't rule people from the grave. Circumstances change and so do attitudes.'

'But you're a Farrell. Doesn't the store mean anything to you?'

'Not much.' Larry faced her squarely. 'Anyway, it hasn't happened yet. This man will only buy me out if he can get your shares too.'

'But that's tantamount to a take-over!' she exclaimed. 'Zachary would be in a minority.' She gave Larry a hard look. 'I would never sell my shares to an outsider.'

'Why not? It would mean a fortune for you.'

'You know how I feel about my shares. I'm holding them in trust for you and Zachary. I'm quite willing to give you half each.'

'What use is that?' Larry said irritably. 'There'd still be stalemate. No one will pay treble for my shares if they're locked into a company which they can't run.' He sighed heavily. 'I knew you wouldn't do it. I've no hard feelings towards you, Samantha. In your position I'd probably do the same.'

She doubted it, but did not say so. After all, there was no point in antagonising him.

'Are you sure you can't do a deal with Zachary?' she ventured. 'Perhaps if you didn't want all the money in one go...'

'I've talked to him until I'm blue in the face, but he refuses to pay my price. The only thing he'll do is——' Larry stopped. 'Anyway, it's no deal.'

'What isn't?'

'Nothing. I'd rather not say any more.'

'You've said too much to stop now. Please tell me, Larry.'

'You won't like it.'

'I'll like it even less if I think you're hiding something. *What* is Zachary willing to do?'

'Give me a high price for a limited number of my shares. Enough to give him control in case *you* decided to sell out to my chappie!'

'He knows I'd never do that,' she said indignantly.

'Zack's a suspicious person. He doesn't have much faith in anyone.'

For the rest of the evening Samantha mulled this over. The more she thought about it, the more determined she became to see Zachary and have it out with him. Had he not been with Marie tonight she would have telephoned him the moment she arrived home; instead she had to be content with the knowledge that she would see him in the morning.

However, the next day she learned he had flown to Paris. Instantly she imagined him there with Marie, a vision that did nothing to set her mind at rest. The day seemed interminably long. She had far too much leisure in which to think and each thought was more mortifying than the last, with Marie featuring in all of them.

Because of this she was taken aback when she saw the girl strolling towards her across the mushroom beige carpet. As always she was exquisitely dressed; her navy and white silk suit exactly matching a navy and white handbag and gloves.

'I didn't know you were working in this department,' Marie said. 'I thought you were still in Dresses.' She fingered a hat on a stand. 'I like this, but it's the wrong colour. Do you have it in blue?'

'I'm afraid not.'

'In white, then. I want something to go with this suit.'

Samantha's eyes moved across the models displayed on the various counters. Suddenly she remembered a beautiful creation that had recently arrived from Milan. The cost would astonish Zachary but, remembering how quick he had been to misjudge her, she was sorry it wasn't double the price.

'You've thought of something for me?' Marie exclaimed. 'I can see it on your face.'

Fervently hoping Marie did not also see the gibbet on which she would have liked to place her, Samantha hurried to the stockroom, returning with a navy straw boater trimmed with white satin roses.

'That's for me,' Marie said promptly, and put it on. 'You know my style exactly, Samantha. I'll always come to you in future.'

She watched the bill made out and then scribbled her name on it. 'You know it goes to Zachary?' she said carelessly.

Samantha nodded and held out her hand for the hat.

'No, no,' Marie said. 'I'm going to wear it. But you can pack my old one. I'm so glad you entertained Zachary while I was in New York,' the French girl continued as Samantha tied the hatbox. 'It stopped me worrying about him.'

'I enjoyed playing the Good Samaritan.'

'I hope you'll continue to be one.'

'Will that be necessary now you are back?' Samantha asked coolly.

'I wasn't suggesting you give Zachary your company,' Marie said abruptly, 'so much as your shares.'

'My *what*?'

Marie's eyes blinked as she saw the look on Samtha's face. 'You don't mean he hasn't asked you yet? From what he said to me yesterday I was under the impression he had. I'm afraid I've spoken out of turn. You'd better forget it.'

'Everybody seems anxious to keep me in the dark

about Zachary and what he wants,' Samantha said bitterly. 'If you don't tell me, I'll ask him myself.'

'You mustn't. He'll be furious with me for being so indiscreet.' There was no doubting the fear in Marie's eyes nor the way she looked over her shoulder, as if afraid Zachary might materialise out of the air.

'Then you'd better tell me,' Samantha repeated.

For an instant tiny white teeth nibbled on Marie's full red lower lip. 'Someone has offered Larry a fantastic price for his shares and Zachary is afraid you'll sell yours too. The day I left for the States he told me he was going to make you an offer for them. That's why I—that's why I didn't hurry right back.'

Any faint hopes Samantha had that Larry had been exaggerating last night died as she heard Marie's story. 'Zachary can't believe I'd sell them to a stranger—no matter what I was offered.'

'In his heart he doesn't believe it,' Marie said instantly. 'He knows how devoted you were to your godfather. But he is a business-man and when it comes to business he can be very hard-headed. That's why he felt he had to—how do you put it—cover things from all angles and make absolutely sure you would do nothing that might put him in an impossible position.'

'They why didn't he openly offer to buy my shares?' Samantha retorted. 'We never even discussed it.'

'Perhaps after he had taken you out a couple of times he might have realised it wasn't necessary,' Marie said softly. 'If you liked him—and he knew it—he probably also knew he had your loyalty.'

Samantha turned away, knowing full well what Marie meant. Once Zachary had taken her out a couple of times he had known she was in love with him and would never do anything that would put him at a disadvantage. No wonder he hadn't mentioned buying the shares. After their first evening together—when she had practically fallen into his arms—he must have decided he had nothing to fear from her. How cleverly he had played his little game; letting her believe she meant something to him. Yes, he was a past master at the art of flirtation, tying her into such an emotional knot that he had been sure not even Larry could straighten her out.

And Larry couldn't have done it either—indeed he had failed to do so last night—but Marie had succeeded instead.

'You do see why Zachary was so upset?' Marie was speaking again, her voice nervous. 'Like you, he believes Farrell's should never be taken over by strangers. But you can't blame him for not being totally sure of your reaction if you were faced with the temptation of a fortune.'

'Yes,' Samantha said dully. 'I do see.'

'And if Larry tells you about these people who want to buy him out,' Marie thrust home the point, 'you wouldn't sell, would you? Not now you know Zachary is so anxious for you not to do so?'

'Your fears for Zachary are commendable,' Samantha said evenly, 'but you don't need to plead on his behalf. He's quite capable of doing so for himself.'

As if sensing she would antagonise Samantha by saying anything more, Marie took the hatbox from her, smiled goodbye and went on her way. But even when she was out of sight Samantha still felt her presence like some malevolent spirit. She did not want to believe what the girl had said, yet she knew it was true. It fitted so perfectly into what Larry had told her last night. How could Zachary have been so cunning? She felt too bitter to be angry and knew that even if she had felt anger, it would have been directed towards herself for having been so easily taken in by him.

Unable to bear serving any more customers, she went down to the staff cloakroom and changed out of her black dress. If only she need never return to Farrell's again! But whether she liked it or not she was still Uncle John's lynch-pin, though at the moment she was so disgusted with Zachary she could well have done what Larry wanted her to do, and sold her shares to the buyer he had mentioned last night.

As this thought came into her mind she frowned. Could Marie have made up the whole story in an effort to cause mischief between herself and Zachary? It would be wonderful if she could believe that. Yet there were several flaws in it; the main one being that Marie, no matter how jealous she was of her, would not wish her to harm Zachary by selling her shares to someone else. 'Perhaps she's hoping I'll be so angry with Zachary that I'll divide my shares between him and Larry and leave Farrell's,' Samantha thought. This seemed such a logical explanation that she immediately decided to go and see Zachary. She would tell him what Marie had said and ask him to tell her the truth. There was nothing she disliked more than prevarication.

Having made her decision she felt much happier, and was feeling almost cheerful by the time she arrived home. Had Zachary not been in Paris she would have telephoned his apartment and gone to see him immediately. Instead she started to think of Marie and Zachary's relationship. Would he go on seeing the French girl now that she was back from America or would his friendship with herself prove to be the more important one? Some of Samantha's cheerfulness ebbed. She knew what Zachary thought and felt when it came to Farrell's, but his innermost emotions were still unknown to her. Morosely she collected some things that needed washing and dumped them into the sink, hoping that physical activity would lessen her mental tension.

As soon as she reached Farrell's the next morning she went to Zachary's office. Mrs Lynton told her he was not returning from Paris until later that morning and, because he had been uncertain of the exact time, had booked no appointments for himself until that afternoon.

'Would you like me to ask him to call you when he gets in?' the woman asked.

Samantha shook her head. 'I'm not sure if I'll be in the Millinery Department. I have to go out on some errands for the buyer. I'll come up again later.'

The errands kept her busy until after midday and by the time she returned to Farrell's it was approaching one o'clock. She debated whether to call Zachary on the telephone, but then decided to go up and see if he was there.

Breathlessly she sped down the corridor to his room and knocked at the outer door. Receiving no reply, she went in. The room was empty and she realised Mrs Lynton had gone to lunch. She hesitated, wondering whether to come back later. But by then Zachary might be too busy to see her.

Quietly she walked across to his office and opened the inner door. It swung back, giving her a view of him standing beside his desk with Marie leaning against him. Their faces were close and Samantha had no doubt that they had been kissing. She felt as if her body had been sharply jarred and went to draw back. Before she could do so, Zachary turned and saw her.

'Samantha!'

He stepped away from Marie. There was no guilt on his face or in his manner, which made Samantha positive he had already decided which one of them he preferred.

Her heart slowed its heavy beat and a great calm came over her.

'If you're busy,' she said, 'I can come back later.'

'That won't be necessary. Marie is just leaving.'

With graceful steps Marie left the room, her skirts brushing Samantha as she moved past her.

'Come in and sit down, Samantha,' Zachary said, and watched as she stepped further into the room. 'It seems a long time since I saw you,' he continued.

'It was only Monday.'

'Well, that's a long time, isn't it? I had to go to Paris unexpectedly. I tried to call you, but I couldn't get hold of you.'

'You don't need to tell me where you are every day of the week.' She could still see the image of Marie in his arms and the sharpness of the memory made her face sharp too.

'I know I don't,' he said, ignoring her tone, 'but I wanted to do so. I've missed you.'

'It looked like it,' she said sarcastically.

A slight smile caused his lower lip to move. Seeing its sensuous curve, she was overcome by jealousy. How dared he look at her like that when only a few moments ago he had been making love to someone else? Knowing she had only herself to blame for Zachary's treatment of her in no way abated her anger.

'I came to see you about my shares,' she said belligerently. 'I understand Larry may sell out to someone else.'

'So he's told you, has he?'

'Well, *you* didn't,' she said bluntly, 'though I can't think why you kept it a secret.'

'I didn't want to talk to you about family matters.'

His words relegated her to the position of a stranger and she felt a spasm of hurt.

'Why won't you buy him out?' she demanded.

'He wants to dispose of his entire holding and I'd have to mortgage myself to the hilt to raise that kind of money.' His expression grew bitter. 'As you know so much, I presume you know he wants treble their market value?'

'They must be worth it,' she replied.

'Worth it or not, I can't find the cash.'

'Can you raise enough to pay treble for my shares? If you bought them you'd at least prevent anyone from having control of the store.'

There was a moment of silence and twin points of light gleamed in the grey eyes watching her. 'I suppose I could find the money to buy *that* number.'

'I thought you could,' she said dryly. 'Was taking me out part of the softening-up process to make sure I didn't go in with Larry?'

The light in his eyes intensified, turning them into silver chips of ice. 'You must believe what you like.'

'I'm asking you to tell me.'

'I have nothing to say.'

Her fury grew. How dared he stand there without defending himself? He had nothing to say because he was guilty. That was what his silence meant.

'I wish Uncle John had never left me those shares,' she burst out. 'I'm sick to death of playing piggy in the middle! The sooner I'm free to leave herc, thc happier I'll be.'

Angrily she rushed from the room, banging the door so hard behind her that the window in the front office rattled.

Too upset to eat lunch, she wandered the streets and then, still overcome by her feelings, went into the park. It was crowded with lunch-time workers eager for a sight of the sun, and she wended her way between groups of chattering girls, huddles of men listening to the latest cricket scores and loving couples sitting close and silent. Bitterly she remembered her Sunday stroll here with Zachary. How cleverly he had made her feel that his liking for her was genuine! He must have been delighted by the way she had succumbed to his charm. When would he have asked her about the shares? Had he been waiting to make sure she was totally besotted over him before doing so? And would he have asked to buy half of them or would he have confidently suggested buying them all? She would never know the answer to that question now.

'Oh, Zachary,' she cried silently, 'how could you be so deceitful?'

Her eyes filled with tears and she blinked her lids. He had been furious when she told him she knew the game he had been playing. The only decent thing he had done was not to try and lie his way out of it.

'Believe what you like,' he had said, which she supposed was better than having him fabricate some story.

The only good thing was that she knew now that Zachary, unlike his cousin, had the interests of Farrell's at heart. In giving him control she could be certain he would never abuse his power nor do anything to endanger the store. With him at the helm, it would remain a family concern and, when he retired, then his own son or daughter would take it over.

Would that be Marie's child? Despairingly Samantha turned away from the question. Zachary meant nothing to her. She must stop thinking about him.

CHAPTER TWELVE

SAMANTHA remembered Zachary telling her Farrell's had a grapevine system second to none when, entering the foyer of her apartment block, she saw Larry waiting for her.

'I hear you and Zachary had a fight this morning,' he said, following her into the lift.

'I had a fight with *him*,' she corrected. 'He considered it beneath his dignity to fight with *me*.' She unlocked her front door and Larry came in and closed it behind her.

'I'm sorry you had to learn about him the hard way, Samantha. I wanted to warn you before, but I knew you wouldn't believe me. You'd have thought it was sour grapes.'

She shrugged. 'They say one only learns through one's own experience.'

'At least he won't be able to fool you again.'

'He won't have the chance. I'm pulling out.'

'Thank heavens you've seen sense! I know you disliked acting as a buffer between Zack and myself, and now at least you've got a chance to get your own back on him.'

'How?'

'By selling to my chappie, of course.'

'I've already said no to that!' She did not attempt to hide her anger. 'I may be disgusted with the way Zachary has behaved, but I still can't go against Uncle John's wishes.'

'Don't be a fool!'

'I'd rather be a fool than——' She caught herself up, realising the futility of repeating how she felt. But one thing she had to say—and the quicker she did it, the better. 'Since Farrell's means so little to you I'm letting Zachary have all my shares. At least then——'

'You're what?' Larry's face contorted with fury. 'That's exactly what he's been angling for. Don't you care that you're playing right into his hands?'

'Of course I care. But I can't do anything else.'

'You could pay him back for the runaround he's given you. Don't you mind being played for a sucker? He had no compunction about ditching Marie for a few weeks in order to try and make you fall in love with him and give him what he wanted. And what do you think he would have done once he'd got his hands on your shares?' Larry flung his arms wide. 'If you want the truth, Samantha, I'll give it to you. Marie was in league with him. That's why she went to the States. She had no real reason to go. That play of her father's was only an excuse. She'd never have left Zack alone with you if he hadn't asked her to do so.'

'It makes no difference to the way I behave,' Samantha said stoically.

'Then I give up! If you're so crazy about him that you don't mind him laughing at you...' Larry strode to the door. 'If you have any pride whatever you'll come in with me and show Zachary there are some things he can't control. Show a bit of spunk, Samantha.'

'I'm thinking of Uncle John, not of myself.'

Samantha put her hands to her temples. Larry opened his mouth, then clamped it shut, the movement signifying that he knew when he had lost.

'Goodbye then,' he said curtly, and slammed the door behind him.

She knew that what Larry had said was right, yet she could not do as he wanted. Much as she wished to hurt Zachary, she could not go against Uncle John's wishes.

Knowing she would have no peace of mind until she had resolved the situation and could return to Ireland, she decided to go back to the store and tell Zachary he must buy her shares immediately. Without bothering to make herself tidy, she ran down to the street and hailed a taxi.

The gleaming façade of Farrell's loomed into sight some ten minutes later and she was about to tell the driver to take her round to the staff door when she stopped herself. There was no need for that; this phase in her life was ending.

The taxi stopped outside the main entrance and she jumped out. As she did so the commissionaire nodded to the driver to remain where he was. He was holding several large dress boxes and a young messenger boy was behind him, carrying four more.

Someone had been on a shopping spree, Samantha thought, and moved towards the entrance. Then hastily she turned her back as she saw Marie heading towards the taxi. So Zachary was going to foot that bill! Even for someone who was notoriously extravagant, the French girl had excelled herself this afternoon. Samantha's anger towards Zachary was exacerbated by this knowledge. It was not envy, she assured herself. It was misery at knowing he cared enough for Marie to pander to her desires.

Trying to forget the episode, she went up to the top floor. Pushing open the door of Mrs Lynton's office, she forced a smile to her face as she said she wanted to see Mr Farrell.

'He won't be able to give you more than a moment,' the woman demurred. 'He's on his way out. I'm not sure he——'

She stopped as the inner door opened and Zachary came through it, halting abruptly as he saw Samantha.

Moistening lips which were unexpectedly dry, Samantha had to swallow hard before she could find her voice. 'I want to—to talk to you, Zachary. It won't take a moment.'

He stepped back and waited for her to precede him into his office before he closed the door. She stared at him coldly and he stared back at her. His crescent-shaped brows met above his eyes, casting a shadow over them which made their expression inscrutable. But his mouth was set in an uncompromising line.

'From the look of your face,' he said, 'I don't think you have come here to apologise to me.'

'I don't owe you an apology.'

A spasm—which could have been anger or irritation—passed swiftly over his face. 'Then why *have* you come here?'

'To tell you that I want to leave for Ireland as soon as possible and that you must buy my shares at once.'

'Are you sure?'

'Sure?' she echoed, not sure what he meant.

'Sure that you do want to sell,' he said. 'Don't do anything in a temper, Samantha. By tomorrow you may regret your decision. Sleep on it and——'

'I don't need to sleep on it. I'm fed up with the whole business and I want to go home. You can have the control you want, and I hope you'll be very happy with it.'

'I'm sure I shall be,' he murmured. 'Although you obviously hate me, I'm glad you're doing the right thing.'

'I don't hate you. I despise you.'

'The sharp tongue has come back again, I see.'

'Not for long,' she retorted. 'When I'm in Ireland you won't be hearing it.'

'You can't leave until you've signed various documents which my lawyer must draw up.'

'Can't they be posted to me?' she asked.

'No. I shall also have to make arrangements for the money.'

'What money?'

An inscrutable expression crossed his face, though his voice remained toneless. 'The money for your shares.'

With a quick intake of breath she went to the door, then with her hand on the knob, looked at him over her shoulder. 'I don't want any money for the shares. Not a penny.'

'Then I won't take them.'

'I'm giving them to you.'

'And I'm refusing them.' His face was hard. 'Since you've made it so clear that you despise me, you can't expect me to accept your charity. You will either let me pay for the shares or you can keep them.'

She thought quickly, then said in a small voice: 'Not treble the value, though. The market price only.'

'Very well.'

She frowned unhappily. 'It will still be an enormous amount of money.'

'I hope you'll spend some of it at Farrell's.' He gave a measured look at her crumpled cotton dress. 'We have an excellent dress department here from which I'm sure you could benefit.'

'If there are any dresses left in it after your girl-friend has finished shopping!'

The side of his mouth lifted in a half smile. 'Be careful what you say, Samantha, or I might think you're jealous.'

'Never of you!' She closed the door behind her and walked blindly to the lift.

The next few days were the longest and most miserable she could remember spending. Peter came round for drinks one evening, but only to tell her he was flying out to New Zealand to see Jackie.

'I miss her,' he confessed, 'and if the only way I can get her back is to marry her, then that's what I'll do.'

'I wouldn't propose to her in those terms,' Samantha warned. 'If Jackie had wanted to snare you she needn't have gone to New Zealand to do it.'

He knew instantly what she meant and gave a half smile. 'As a matter of fact I *want* to marry that madcap friend of yours. I can't even rustle up enough interest in another girl to take one out. And coming from me, that's some admission.'

'How long are you going for?' she asked.

'A month. I'm hoping we'll make it our honeymoon. You can give us our wedding present on our return!'

'I'll have to send it to you from Ireland. I'm going back home.'

'And this place?'

Her eyes widened. 'Of course. What a fool I am for not thinking of it myself. I'd be delighted for you to take it over.'

'Done.' He gave her a curious look. 'How come you're returning to the land of peat and bog? I thought you were having a ball here.'

'The ball is over.'

Peter was astute enough to sense her reluctance to say more, and he finished his drink and made his farewells.

By Monday Samantha was ready to leave London. She longed to disregard Zachary's instructions, and only because she didn't want him to know she was running away from him did she heed them.

Each time the telephone rang she expected it to be a message from his lawyers, but it was five o'clock before they called to say the documents would be ready for her signature the following afternoon. She longed to ask the voice at the other end of the line if Zachary would be there too, but with a great effort she held back the question.

However, the following day she dressed for her appointment with great care. After his disparaging remarks about her appearance she intended to look her best, and knew that her beige linen suit was a perfect foil for her colouring, making her look as cool and delicious as a coffee ice. She looked at herself a long time in the mirror, wishing her slender curves were more voluptuous and that her long soft hair was dark and wavy. She knew she was being ridiculous and that in her own way she was equal in looks to Marie. Yet this did little for her peace of mind, for it was the curvaceous brunette whom Zachary preferred.

Like a mirage he rose in front of her: dark and virile and wide of shoulder, which made him appear taller than he was. What comfort a girl would find against that broad, strong chest and what happiness in those firm but tender arms. Quickly she looked away from her reflection, afraid that the sight of her haunted eyes would only add to her sadness, though she was in complete control of herself when she entered the offices of Zachary's lawyers.

The first words from the senior partner told her that Zachary would not be coming. 'But all the documents are ready for your signature, Miss Byers,' he went on, and led her across to a chair beside his desk.

She sat down and stared at the red-ribboned parchment sheets before her. 'Where do I sign?' she asked.

'Don't you want to read them?'

'Is my entire holding being made over to Zachary Farrell?' she asked.

'He is buying them from you at market price.'

She let out her breath on a deep sigh, then picked up a

pen and quickly signed her name on all the documents. 'Is that all?' she asked.

'Yes.'

'Good.' She went to the door, stopping as he called her name.

'You've forgotten your cheque from Mr Farrell.'

The lawyer handed her a sealed envelope and she slipped it into her bag, gave him another perfunctory smile and left the office.

She was aware that the lawyer thought her extremely abrupt, but she had found it impossible to make casual conversation with him when all she wanted to do was to burst into tears. Sooner or later she would forget Zachary. It was knowing that he was so close that was making it hard for her. Once she was in Ireland, she would start to see him in perspective.

The journey back to Sloane Street was slow, with traffic thick as clotted cream. The taxi meter ticked on unmercifully and, looking at the fare, she suddenly realised it didn't matter. Despite her misery she now had a great deal of money. She frowned at the knowledge. What would she do with it? It was a question that was not difficult to answer, for in her present frame of mind she knew she would never be able to spend it. She would leave it in the bank. She might even go and talk to another lawyer and see if there was a way of giving it back to Zachary. When his temper had cooled he might be willing to accept its return.

She took the envelope from her bag and opened it. There was a thick sheet of writing paper inside it but no cheque: only a letter written in Zachary's hand.

'I cannot accept the shares,' he began abruptly, 'and certainly not at the price you wanted me to pay, for they are worth considerably more. If you still wish me to have them at a later stage, I suggest we talk about it.

In the meantime my lawyer has instructions to destroy the documents you signed and for the share certificates to remain in your name. I do not believe—and never did—that you would sell your shares to the highest bidder. If you had been that sort of a person, you would have fallen in with Larry's plans. However, you are still free to do so, if you wish. You see I am putting myself in your hands, which shows that I have greater trust in you than you have in me.'

Numbly Samantha re-read the letter, not fully comprehending it. How could Zachary trust her the way he had said? Didn't he know that by giving her back her shares she could put him in a most difficult position at Farrell's? She wondered what Larry would say if he knew of Zachary's behaviour and vowed he would never find out from her.

She was still uncertain what to do when she had paid the taxi and went up to her flat. Despite everything she had done to be rid of all responsibility, she was now back where she had started. Yet she was determined not to have any part in running the store. She would have someone to stand in for her and hope that eventually Zachary would buy her out. Dejectedly she paced the floor. What did he hope to gain by refusing her offer, and what was he trying to prove by saying he trusted her? It could only be his way of sneering at her for not having trusted him.

Abruptly she sat down. How would she feel if she discovered that she *had* misjudged him? The thought was too bitter to contemplate and she shied away from it, knowing full well that before the evening was out she would have to ask Zachary to explain the reasons behind his action.

Refusing to give herself more time to brood, she dialled his home. The bell rang several times before she heard his voice. As always its deepness set her pulse tingling and she tried not to visualise him at the other end of the line, standing dark and aloof amidst the quietness of his beige and cream living-room.

'I got your letter,' she said in a trembling voice. 'I think you're being ridiculous.'

'I'm sorry. But it was the only way I could prove that I have trust in you.'

'Why do you want to prove that?'

'Because it's also the only way of telling you that I didn't make love to you in order to get you to favour me instead of Larry.'

'Why did you do it, then?' She thought of Marie and was goaded into temper. 'Was I a stand-in for your girlfriend?'

There was a long silence. 'Goodbye, Samantha,' he said at last. 'I don't think we have anything more to say.'

'You're right,' she said shakily, and put down the receiver.

Only then did she take out his letter again and re-read it, seeing how her accusations must have hurt him for him to have done this most extraordinary thing. No wonder his lawyer had looked at her strangely when he had given her the envelope. He had probably thought his client was mad: going to the pretence of having him prepare documents which—once she had signed them—he had instructions to tear up.

She unzipped her dress and went into the bedroom. She longed to curl up on her bed and pull the blankets over her head, but she resisted the temptation. She would have a bath first. The hot water might ease the tension that was making her nerves taut and her temples ache. As the water ran she switched on the radio, then soaking in the steamy depths, she concentrated on the banal words of the latest pop song.

Pink-skinned, she finally emerged from the bath and, wrapped in a long, fleecy robe, padded into the kitchen to try to quell the queasy pangs in her stomach. She opened the refrigerator and stared at a packet of butter and a carton of croissants. It wasn't much, but it was better than nothing. She was about to take them out when she saw a half bottle of champagne on the bottom shelf. That was a much better idea. It would at least stop her feeling sorry for herself.

Gingerly she unwrapped the gold foil. There was a loud pop and the cork flew into the air. Champagne foamed over the edge of the bottle and she quickly tipped it into a glass. Holding the glass and the half empty bottle in her hand, she headed towards the living-room.

She was crossing the hall when there was a tattoo on the door. She looked at it apprehensively, remembering all the dangers that could befall girls who lived alone in a big city.

'Who is—who's there?' she called loudly.

'Zachary.'

She backed away from the door almost as if she could see through it.

'Open up,' he said. 'I don't intend to talk to you through a panel of wood.'

'I don't want to talk to you.'

His knuckles rapped on the door again and she moved across and opened it. Instantly he stepped through, as if afraid she would slam it on him.

He seemed much taller, until she recollected that she was not wearing any shoes. Nor was she wearing any clothes beneath her robe. Nervously she went to tighten the belt. The bottle of champagne slipped and she grasped it. Sensing her dilemma, Zachary stepped forward and tightened the belt for her, then he eyed her from the top of her damp head to the pink toes peeping beneath the white towelling.

'Expecting someone?'

'Not you,' she said promptly.

'Pity.'

She moved back a step and took a gulp of champagne. 'What do you want? I haven't got time to stand here talking to you.' There was no doubting the amusement in his face and she knew he was laughing at her. 'I suppose you think it was funny having me sign those documents and then making arrangements for them to be torn up?'

'It was the only possible thing I could do in the circumstances.' He walked into the sitting-room. 'If you have another glass,' he said conversationally, 'you could offer me some champagne. That's something I *am* willing to take from you.'

'Help yourself,' she said shortly, and held out the bottle.

He took it and the tips of his fingers touched hers. She let go of the bottle. It slipped and with an exclamation he bent and caught it.

'You're very nervous of me, Samantha.'

'How do you expect me to feel? You're the last person in the world I want to see.'

'I'm afraid you're stuck with me for the next few minutes. I've come to say something and I don't intend to leave until I've said it.'

'Then be quick about it. I have a date.'

'With whom?'

'That's none of your business.'

'Well, at least I can keep you company until he arrives.'

She thought wildly. 'He isn't arriving. I—I'm meeting him in the West End.'

'Then I'll take you there.'

'Peter wouldn't like that,' she said, glad she had suddenly remembered him. 'He's very jealous.'

'Peter?' For the first time Zachary looked perturbed.

'Peter Jackson, the photographer,' she explained. 'I'm sure you've heard of him.'

'Isn't he the man your friend was hoping to marry?'

'That was in the past,' Samantha said, marvelling at his memory. 'He's *my* boy-friend now.'

'Stop it, Samantha,' Zachary said in such a loud voice that she jumped like a startled doe.

'S-stop what?'

'Stop pretending that you have another date. I don't believe you.'

'Really? Did you imagine I would moon over you for the next six months?'

'I would like to think you would moon over me for far longer than that.' He set down his glass and, reaching across, did the same with hers. Then he put both hands on her arms. 'Come here, Samantha.'

She ignored him and he pulled her roughly forward. The sash of her robe loosened and the towelling parted. He caught his breath sharply, then with trembling fingers pulled the robe closely around her.

'I love you, Samantha,' he said huskily, and held her against his chest. She struggled within his hold, but he would not let her go. 'Be careful,' he warned, 'your sash is still on the floor.'

Instantly she became as motionless as a statue. 'You're a beast to take advantage of me like this!'

'Considering I re-wrapped you in your fleecy coverall, I can hardly be accused of taking advantage of you!'

'Well, at least let me go to my room and put on something else.'

'And run the risk of having you lock the door on me?'

Since this was exactly what she had intended to do, she gave him full marks for deducing it. 'Please, Zachary,' she whispered, 'say what you have to say and then go.'

'I love you,' he repeated. 'I took you out because I wanted to be with you.'

'Marie is your girl-friend.'

'Only until I fell in love with *you*.'

'At first sight, no doubt,' Samantha said sarcastically.

'No,' he said, 'I won't lie about that. At our first meeting I could cheerfully have strangled you.' He paused, and his hands moved down her back and came to rest on her waist. 'I think it was when you knocked that dummy over in the dress department and its head landed at my feet. You looked like a little girl whose doll had broken. I knew then that I wasn't going to get you out of my mind.'

'You never gave any indication of it.'

Her voice was muffled because he was holding her so close that her face was pressed against his chest. His jacket was undone and she felt the silkiness of his shirt and was surprised that it was slightly damp. This, more than anything else, was indicative of the emotions he was trying so hard to hide. But there were many emotions that a man could feel for a woman, and most of them had nothing to do with love.

'Please, Zachary, let me go. I can't talk to you unless I can see you.' The quietness of her voice seemed to satisfy him that she was prepared to be sensible, and he released her.

'Well, Samantha, will you let me finish what I started?'

'What did you start?'

'What I hoped was going to be a lifetime love affair with you. I love you and I want to marry you.'

'As well as have Marie for a girl-friend? I know she only went to America because you asked her to go.'

His astonished look changed to one of comprehension, and with it his whole demeanour altered. His eyes darkened with anger and the well-shaped mouth grew thin and tight. 'When did she tell you that?'

'The day you were in Paris.'

'How could you have believed her?' he asked quietly. 'I thought I'd made it so plain the way I felt about you.'

'Because you kissed me? You never said anything.'

'I didn't think words were necessary. Besides, I was afraid you might think I was being nice to you because of those damned shares of yours. And of course Marie was clever enough to know what was in my mind.'

'How did you plan to overcome my suspicions?'

'I was hoping to buy Larry's shares—or at least enough of them to give me the control I needed—without involving you. Unfortunately Larry was only willing to sell his entire holding and I couldn't afford the price.'

'Then why have you given my shares back to me?' she demanded. 'That means you still don't have control.'

'Because it's the only way I can show you that I trust you. I meant what I said in that letter, Samantha. I know you will never do anything to harm Farrell's or me—which is more than I can say of my cousin.' There was an unusual note of bitterness in Zachary's voice. 'I know he's keen to put this invention of his to the test, but he has no need to set such a high price on his shares.'

'Larry doesn't have the same loyalties as you,' Samantha said. 'He also implied that Marie stayed in America because you had asked her to do so.'

'Poor Larry, he really was prepared to do anything to get things his own way.'

'What do you think he'll do now?' she asked. 'The

man who wants to buy him out will only do so if he can have my shares too.'

'Larry won't be stuck for long,' Zachary said dryly. 'He'll either be prepared to do a deal with me or put his engineering project into cold storage. Anyway, whatever he does is unimportant as long as I have you.'

Once again he drew her close. This time she did not resist him, but lay in the haven of his arms with a deep content.

'Even when I thought I hated you,' she whispered, 'I could never have done anything to hurt you.'

'I knew that, my darling.' His voice was deeper than she had ever heard it. 'I only have myself to blame for you misunderstanding me. I should have told you I was trying to negotiate with Larry, but I hated talking business to you. I didn't want to involve you in all the trouble I was having.'

'I'm sure the two of us can get him to behave decently.'

'I don't care what he does,' Zachary said fiercely. 'All I'm concerned with is you.' He looked into her upturned face and recognised the question lurking in the depths of her eyes. 'Still worried about Marie?'

'Only because she's so recent. And you did rush to meet her at the airport.'

'You could call that a guilty conscience. You see, I'd made it clear I wanted to end my friendship with her. That's why she went to the States. She kept telephoning me while she was there and begged me to meet her at the airport. I thought that was as good a time as any to make it quite clear that everything was over between us.'

'No wonder she had a go at me the following day!'

'You poor darling,' Zachary said tenderly, and then gave her a shake, 'but more fool you for believing her.'

He went to kiss her, but she turned her head sharply. 'What is it?' he asked.

She hesitated, trying to think of a diplomatic way of putting her final doubts into words, but it was impossible to be diplomatic in these circumstances and bluntly she said: 'You can't have made your feelings all that clear to Marie. I saw her on Friday coming out of Farrell's with half the Dress Department.'

Zachary looked stupefied, then he gave a wry grin. 'That's exactly the sort of thing Marie would do. Don't you see why she went on a shopping splurge? She knew that once I had a chance to attend to my personal things I would close her account. Being Marie, she thought she would replenish her wardrobe first.' Again he shook with laughter.

'You won't find it so funny when you get the bill.'

'I'll charge it up to experience.' He nuzzled his face into the side of Samantha's neck and breathed in the scent of her. 'Don't let's waste time talking about unimportant people when all I want to do is to talk about you and our future. How long will you keep me waiting?'

'For what?' she asked provocatively.

'For marriage and your beautiful body!'

'I like the order in which you put it!' She rubbed her lips down the side of his cheek. 'If only you'd said this to me weeks ago I would have saved myself such a lot of unhappiness.'

'Me too,' he said grimly. 'But Larry kept telling me how suspicious you were of me...'

'You mean he did a Marie on you?'

'I'm afraid so. We were both rather stupid, but from now on that's all in the past.' He sought her lips and at the same time his hands moved down her towelling robe to press her body hard against his. 'It might be a good idea if you did put some clothes on,' he said. 'Otherwise you could prove too much of a temptation to me.'

'You must learn to resist temptation.' She spoke against his mouth. 'Farrell's isn't a monastery and there are lots of pretty girls walking around there.'

'Once you came into my life I had eyes for no one else. You've spoiled me for any other woman, Samantha. Not just because you're beautiful but because you're honest and intelligent. You have me hooked. So the sooner you marry me the sooner I'll be out of my misery.'

'We both live in the same parish,' she said lightly. 'All you have to do is get the banns called.'

'Nothing will stop me.'

His mouth became warmer upon hers and, as its pressure increased, the misunderstandings faded. The only reality was being in Zachary's arms; there was her future and her happiness.